Saffron's CHOICE

Caroline Bell Foster

LMH PUBLISHING LIMITED

Editor: Tyrone S. Reid
Cover Design: Sanya Dockery
Cover Illustration: Terry Grundle
Typeset & Book layout: Sanya Dockery
Author's Photograph: Brian Bell

Published by: LMH Publishing Limited
Suite 10-11
LOJ Industrial Complex
7 Norman Road
Kingston C.S.O., Jamaica
Tel.: (876) 938-0005; 938-0712
Fax: (876) 759-8752
Email: lmhbookpublishing@cwjamaica.com
Website: www.lmhpublishing.com

Printed in the U.S.A   ISBN: 978-976-8202-74-1

NATIONAL LIBRARY OF JAMAICA CATALOGUING IN PUBLICATION DATA

Foster, Caroline
    Saffron's Choice / Caroline Bell Foster

        p. ; cm.

    ISBN 978-976-8202-74-1 (pbk)

    1.   Jamaican Fiction   I.   Title

    813   dc 22

Chapter One

$\mathscr{I}$'s the kind of place frequented by young professionals. A place where the rose and the squiggly tree are debated with such vigour and camaraderie that the large room could be divided into for and against by the patrons who come here to drink gallons of exotic coffee.

No alcohol is served, yet the place thrives better than the over three hundred or so night spots that make Nottingham's city centre one of the best clubbing areas in the East Midlands.

No Worries is actually the bar's official name, but most people simply call it Lucas's place. It's a hugely successful coffee bar filled with red leather sofas so deep and plush they make you feel completely weightless. Shiny espresso machines and highly polished brass fittings give the otherwise dark room a spot of shimmer and shine.

Taking a quick glance at his reflection in one of the huge and heavily gilded mirrors across the room, Lucas checked his appearance and again made a mental note to get his hair cut. He quickly pushed the hair out of his eyes with long, clean, impatient fingers.

Picking up the steaming mug of sweet black coffee he'd carefully brewed for Cassidy, he walked across the gleaming, dark wooden floor with long assured strides, oblivious to the women closely watching his every move and salivating over his good looks.

Lucas had jet black hair with a slight wave, unusual burnished gold eyes and strong chiselled features. He was tall, well over six feet, lean, broad-shouldered and unconsciously carried an air of charisma and commanding arrogance that men wanted to emulate and women longed to investigate. Lucas could have any woman he wanted, and he did, on occasion, but his heart belonged to only one.

Placing the coffee mug on a low, chunky mahogany table, he cast an eye over the room, making sure all the tables were clean and his customers relaxed and happy.

As the owner, he allowed himself that small dose of pride as, like a lord, he watched over the place. He knew most of the customers on a first name basis and prided himself on remembering little details about them.

With a glance at the large antique clock behind the bar, he signalled one of the waitresses to bring over the small mixed platter of spicy chicken wings, samosa and onion rings he'd already prepared, knowing Cassidy and Saffron would be walking in at any moment.

Every Wednesday night for the past fifteen months, the two girls, friends since childhood, came to No Worries to catch up. Lucas knew Saffron since university. They did their business degrees together and had later opened new businesses within weeks of each other. He operated this coffee bar while she ran a hugely successful shop called The Mother Lode in the large shopping mall across town. She sold an eclectic mix of exotic treasures — from jewellery, scarves and bags to cushions and handicrafts mainly from North Africa and Eastern Asia.

Cassidy came in first and Lucas struggled hard not to appear alarmed at how she looked. Deep marks of exhaustion formed under her blue-grey eyes, and her narrow shoulders slumped forward. She looked about ready to drop. But Cassidy being Cassidy, would never let anyone catch her, and Lucas knew this.

He stood politely as she reached him, and with an outstretched arm indicated for her to precede him out onto the cobbled patio. Although it was late October the weather had been unusually mild this past week, and a few of the customers were outdoors enjoying the ambience, watching the colourful canal boats as they glided silently past.

"How've you been, Cass?" he enquired as he placed the black coffee in front of her and the food platter in the centre of the table as they sat down.

"I'm as fine as I could be, Lucas," she admitted, with a slight shrug of her bony shoulders. He watched as she lifted the steaming mug to her lips, blew on it lightly and took a sip of the hot liquid.

"Mm, just right as usual. Thanks," she said.

Cassidy worked hard. She spent hours doing double, sometimes triple, shifts at the bakery where she worked, just outside of town, before going on to do a midnight-to-five shift at a packing factory located on an industrial estate.

When she slept Lucas didn't know, and he just couldn't understand why she worked so hard when she had no responsibilities apart from rent and the usual bills. But then, he suspected, there was a lot more to Cassidy Gaunton than he knew.

She was cold, vague and distant to the point of rudeness to just about everyone, except him and Saffron, and she carried a load of secrets on her tiny shoulders. His heart ached at the sight of her hands clasped around the heavy white mug; her knuckles were red and swollen, her nails bitten almost to the quick, her long blonde hair pulled back into a tight bun that still had the compulsory black hair net from the bakery covering it. He wanted to help her, had offered to help her, but, to his frustration, she wouldn't let him.

A large group of noisy, young Med students got up to leave. They waved and nodded goodbye to Lucas as they made their way to the exit. He watched with amusement as the men in the group fell silent and parted like the Red Sea to let someone through. He was not surprised to see Saffron.

It was always like that. Saffron was gorgeous, all polish and gloss. At five feet ten inches, she commanded admiring glances and stunned stares. Yet she rarely, if ever, played up her good looks. Tonight she had on dark boot-cut jeans, high-heeled black boots, which put her over six feet, and a burnt orange skinny jumper that complimented her honey brown complexion. Tonight she was feeling good. Lucas knew this by the false ponytail she wore. She had a collection, ranging in colours and styles. Tonight's was straight, dark and ran down to her waist. Last week's had fiery red tips. She'd been in a seriously bad mood then, Lucas recalled with amusement.

As usual, a familiar heat stole through his body whenever she was near. He fought hard to tame the fiery desire that burned for her inside him. She was his friend and he valued their friendship too much to ever do anything to satisfy the lust that raged inside his body.

"Latte on the rocks, Lucas, please," Saffron ordered with her usual sassiness, as she leaned into him to receive her customary kiss on the cheek. Only Cassidy, watching on with envy at their closeness, noticed the way Lucas's nostrils flared and his hands tightened into fists just before he gathered Saffron in his arms for a close hug.

⁂

As Lucas sauntered off to get the latte, Saffron sat in his chair, leaned across and hugged Cassidy.

"You're not looking well, Cass," Saffron said with the straight-forward concern Cassidy was used to. "In fact, you look worse than last week. You can't keep on like this," she warned, her dark brown eyes casting a frowning glance at her friend's gauntness.

"You know why I'm doing this," Cassidy replied, sounding tired. "I've got to find him, Saff. Everywhere I look I see moms with their kids. My son's out there somewhere looking for me. I know he is. I can feel it in here." She pressed a bony fist to her heart. Her large blue-grey eyes shimmered with tears, and Saffron reached across to take her free hand.

"I know, but at what cost? You're running yourself to the ground, Cass. Burning yourself out. At least take a few days off," Saffron suggested, though already predicting the answer.

"I can't. With every day that passes, he slips further and further away from me. I can't afford to stop. I will never stop," said Cassidy.

Lucas, feeling the throbbing emotion at the table, gave Saffron her latte and silently slipped back to the bar.

"It's been a long time, Cass," Saffron whispered.

"Do you think I don't know that?" Cassidy replied sobbing, her eyes darkening with pain and despair. "Eleven years since I held him, Saff. Eleven years!" She covered her face with hands that shook as she tried in vain to hide her distress.

"Cassidy," Saffron pressed. "Cass?"

Cassidy hastily wiped the tears from her eyes and looked at her. Cassidy hated to break down, especially in front of someone.

"Has the private investigator found anything new to go on?" Saffron asked.

"Nothing more than last week," Cassidy replied, sniffing. "He knows Tarif's family lives in Bolton, but Tarif hasn't been there in months and months. Nobody is talking, Saffron! They all close ranks, protecting their own, even when they know he's done bad. I hate them, Saff!" Cassidy pounded a bony fist on the table, making a trickle of froth from Saffron's drink slip over the edge of her mug. "All of them!" Cassidy added, the anger and hatred burning deep within her.

Saffron didn't know what to do or say. It was a heart-wrenching story, every mother's worst nightmare: Giving birth to a child, loving that child for a few short months before he is snatched away by its own father, no less, never to be seen again. Cassidy had exhausted all leads. Her son, Billal, had seemingly disappeared off the face of the earth. Cassidy's desperate frustration was understandable. Her burning hatred scary. Saffron wished she could do more to help.

"The investigator did say he thinks he may have to go to India though, as Tarif's family have large holdings there," Cassidy said, again in control of her emotions. "I'll have to pay for all his expenses. I've got no choice," she added, shrugging dolefully.

"I'll give you the money, Cass. You know I will. You don't have to do it alone."

"I know and I thank you," Cassidy said, smiling weakly. "You've been a good friend to me, Saff. Remember at school when that boy, what was his name? Ashley something or the other, and he used to bully me, pulling my hair and calling me a benefit baby, making me cry, and you got him by the neck in the playground and made him apologise?"

Saffron smiled and nodded at the almost twenty-year-old memory.

"I promised myself I'd do anything for you. And now, years later, I still rely on you. I'm still a burden!" said Cassidy.

"Don't be ridiculous. We're friends. Friends don't get gold stars from each other for being true friends, tallying them up each year!" Saffron admonished heatedly. "I'm here for you, and I promise to always be here for you."

Cassidy smiled a watery smile. She'd been crying a lot lately and she had to stop it, she told herself sternly. Being weak was not going to get Billal back.

"Thanks, Saff. You're too good to me. Have you spoken to that boyfriend of yours lately?"

Saffron grinned. "Last night. His mother isn't very well and going to need surgery and I can tell you any kind of hospitalisation in Jamaica will cost. So I'm sending some more money out."

"Any idea when he'll come over?"

Saffron sighed, picked up an onion ring and bit into it before answering. "His passport hasn't come through yet, but hopefully he'll be here in the New Year."

Cassidy refrained from reminding Saffron that she'd said the same thing this time last year, and probably the year before that too.

The girls chatted and finished their drinks, each enjoying the other's company as only lifelong friends could.

"I'm doing an extra shift at the factory tonight," Cassidy said some time later as she looked across to the bar, noting the time and the busty blonde latching onto Lucas's arm. "In fact, I'd better be going."

"I'll take you to work," Saffron offered, getting up.

"No, no, no, there'll be a staff bus leaving in twenty minutes, just outside the train station." Cassidy nabbed the last chicken wing, gave Saffron a quick hug and made to rush off. "But thanks anyway."

"Hey Cass!" Lucas shouted as she was about to walk past. She stopped, noting the way the blonde he'd been talking to looked her up and down and dismissed her with obvious distaste. Cassidy lifted her chin and marched over.

"This is for you." Lucas pushed a paper bag into her startled hands before she could even see what it was. She looked down at the clear plastic containers filled with goodies and the bright green No Worries napkins stuffed inside. For a moment Cassidy stood staring at it, moved beyond belief at Lucas's generosity.

Cassidy looked up at Lucas, and in the fleeting moment, their eyes met. She knew he understood. She didn't say thanks as she turned to leave, as he'd already read it in her eyes.

❧ ❦ ❧ ❦

Saffron relaxed into her chair and nibbled on the corner of a spicy samosa. Closing her eyes, she allowed herself to sink into the luxury of the silent night.

She was alone as everyone had either left or moved inside. She enjoyed her Wednesday evenings with Cassidy and never missed one as she knew Cassidy depended on them as much for moral support as she did to keep a close eye on her friend.

Saffron had been living in Jamaica at the time doing her exams when Cassidy first met Tarif. Cassidy had sent letter after letter about this handsome man who'd asked her to marry him and whom she'd planned to change her religion for.

At the time, Saffron had been caught up in a whirlwind romance of her own and was happy for her friend. It wasn't until Cassidy wrote about the pregnancy that Saffron became truly worried. Within months of announcing her news, the letters stopped coming and Saffron's letters returned unopened. Months later, and back in England, Cassidy, desperate and near collapse, had found her again. Tarif had stolen the baby and vanished.

A high-pitched giggle interrupted Saffron's reverie, and she opened her eyes to see a tiny blonde sitting on a stool by the bar, laughing with Lucas. It was hard to miss him tonight, Saffron thought with an affectionate smile, noticing his pleated chocolate-coloured leather trousers that only a man who was comfortable with himself could pull off and a green, long-sleeved silk shirt that reminded her of creamy pistachio ice-cream in Jamaica.

Saffron shifted in her chair and closed her eyes again, wanting to recapture the tranquility. Her thoughts moved to her own problems. It saddened her to finally accept that if it wasn't for the pictures scattered about her flat, she would have great difficulty remembering her boyfriend Roderick's smiling face.

She'd been feeling an urgency she couldn't explain lately and had to ring him everyday for reassurance. It had been four years since she'd last seen him, and it was only for a week. They had barely spent any-time alone together as he'd been working, and his brothers and sisters were always about. It had been difficult and she had left feeling slightly dejected and unfulfilled.

The high-pitched giggle screeched across Saffron's nerves again, and she opened her eyes to see the blonde now practically on top of the counter, pushing her breasts into Lucas's face. It was as comical as it was pitiful. And Lucas, she noted with a frisson of annoyance, had his arm around her shoulders and seemed quite taken with the view.

Picking up her empty mug, Saffron made her way behind the bar as she knew how to work the gleaming apparatus almost as well as

Lucas, and with a smile in their direction, proceeded to help herself to a mug of hot chocolate.

"Everything all right, Saff?" Lucas asked. She nodded and turned to face them, a slight smile playing at the corner of her mouth. The blonde, she noticed, looked put out as Lucas removed his arm and turned his back to her.

"I see you can have an early night tonight," Saffron pointed out as she glanced around the empty room. She watched with satisfaction as a touch of red crept up Lucas's neck when he quickly swung around, noticing for the first time that his customers and staff had left.

"Well, um, I guess," he said.

"You finish doing what you're doing," Saffron said to the girl with a slight nod. "And I'll start to lock up." She patted Lucas on the arm and left them to it with a knowing wink.

Almost half an hour later Lucas came back inside alone. He'd apparently said his goodbyes privately. Saffron furiously noted the smear of bright red lipstick around his mouth.

Silently, together they wiped the tables, removed the last of the mugs, cups and platters into the kitchen, stacked them in the dishwasher and turned it on. The rhythmic whooshing was comfortably familiar. Saffron could do all this with her eyes closed. She felt as at home here as she did at her own flat.

"Lucas?" she called softly when everything was tidy. "Do you want a hot chocolate or something else?"

"Whatever you're having," he replied as he switched off all but one of the lights before moving to a sofa and sitting down, stretching his long, leather-clad legs out and crossing them at the ankles. With a contented grunt he closed his eyes.

"Here you go." Saffron placed the hot drink on the low table in front of him before sitting down, her knees touching his thigh as she curled her legs under herself. They'd spent many a night just like this, talking and drinking hot chocolate. Lucas had his rich and sweet with tiny marshmallows. Lucas was her best friend, and they'd been through many nights of cramming for exams, planning, dreaming and laughing together. He knew her like no other, and she loved him for it.

He opened his eyes and turned to look at her, shifting slightly so as not to touch her.

"Cassidy doesn't look well, Saff," he stated with a concerned frown. "In fact, she looks about ready to drop, and before you say anything, I know you won't tell me what's going on, but at least assure me she's not on drugs."

"No drugs, but she's in a desperate situation. I just don't know what she'll do next."

"It's bloody frustrating," he said, dragging a hand through his long hair, "watching her fade away like this and not being able to help her."

"I know. I feel as though she is close to doing something though, Lucas, and all I can do is keep an eye on her, and make sure she doesn't do anything stupid."

Saffron leaned forward to get her drink and Lucas struggled not to look at the slight curve of her small breasts with the prominent nipples. She wasn't wearing a bra again, he noticed, and he tried hard not to imagine her deliciously naked nipples against his tongue.

"Come here, Lucas," Saffron ordered, breaking into his heated thoughts. He fought to clear his head and focus on her face. "I'll only bite if you want me to." She teased him, completely unaware of how her words enflamed him. His eyes flickered gold, but he leaned towards her so close he could feel the warmth of her breath on his cheek and smell her sweet scent. She licked a finger and rubbed it roughly against the side of his mouth.

"Ouch! What are you doing? And can you rub any harder?" he complained with deep sarcasm. He needed to get away from her. He bit his tongue hard, trying to deflect the painful throb of his arousal before she noticed the hard length of it.

"Don't be such a baby," Saffron mocked.

Lucas stilled, his golden eyes flashing a warning glint she ignored, completely unimpressed by it. He could be so incredibly stuffy sometimes.

"You've got trashy red lipstick all over you. Having problems finding her mouth, Lucas?" she taunted playfully.

He jerked her hand off him and held it tight. "Don't." He looked at her through darkened narrowed eyes.

"What's the matter with you?" she asked aloud as she tugged to get her hand out of his hard clasp.

For a brief moment he tightened his grip then flung her hand away as he got up and moved towards the window with his back to her. His body was rigid, she noticed, his hands stuffed into his trendy trouser pockets, the brown leather stretched tautly across his firm bum.

"What the hell was that?" Saffron asked, rubbing her sore hand.

If anything, Lucas's back stiffened even more.

"I'm sorry," he muttered.

"What was that? An apology?" Saffron watched with intrepid fascination as he slowly took his hands out of his pockets to flex his fingers. She'd never seen him like this. What was the matter with him?

"Look, I didn't mean to hurt you."

"Me or the window?" she joked, wanting desperately to lighten the mood.

He turned, pinning her to the sofa with his glare. "Can't you be serious for one damn minute?"

"Lucas, so you forgot your strength? I'll live," she replied in shock, as he'd never spoken to her like that before. She stood, picked up their half-empty mugs, and went into the kitchen to rinse them out. The dish washer had stopped.

"Leave that," he said from the doorway as he watched her soap a mug, rinse it under the tap and turn it upside down onto the metal draining board.

"We always tidy up," she replied tightly, striving for normality through the throbbing silence.

"I said leave it!" Lucas gritted through his clenched teeth.

Wide-eyed, Saffron slowly breathed in and out, put the green soapy sponge down, turned off the tap and began to pull off one yellow rubber glove, finger by finger.

She turned to face him. "Don't be taking your frustrations out on me if your new girlfriend went home without you tonight!"

Lucas's mouth flattened, his eyes flashed yellow. "She's not my girlfriend, and you would know a lot about frustrations, wouldn't you, sweetheart?" he mocked cruelly. "A boyfriend you haven't seen in what? Five years?"

"It's four actually and you know why. He can't get a passport!"

"And how lame is that." He moved towards her. Trapping her in place with his eyes. She felt like a captured butterfly fluttering frantically but getting nowhere. "Jamaica may be a Third World country, but I'm sure even they could manage to process a passport in a couple of weeks."

"How would you know?" she whispered, hurt beyond belief at his savage cruelty.

"I know that good ol' Roderick doesn't want to come here. I know that that boyfriend of yours is taking you for a ride, honey." His lips curled cruelly as he leaned his face close to hers, their noses almost touching. "How much money has he taken from you this month?"

Her chin went up and she struggled hard not to show how much pain he was causing her. "None! But so what if I send money over. He's got a big family and they're not exactly well off. They can do a lot over there with even a couple of pounds!" She didn't like the way Lucas's mouth twisted with derision. "And so what!" she continued. "It's my money, my life I can do what I want with it. At least I have one man in my life. You don't keep a girlfriend for longer than two weeks!" She poked a gloved finger into his hard chest. "You think you can lecture me about my life, when yours is filled with scatter-brained bimbos with rubber boobs to their chins and legs to their eyebrows!"

"That's enough, Saffron," Lucas warned sternly.

"No, it's not enough!" She poked him again. "How can you judge me when it's you who hasn't had a decent relationship since I've known you? So don't you dare preach to me about my li—"

Before she could finish, Lucas pinned her against the sink, and with a deep throated growl covered her mouth with his. Shocked, she opened her mouth, and he took advantage to sweep inside with his tongue.

Saffron felt the hardness of his body as he pressed into her, the rigidity of his hard arousal against her narrow hip. He moved a hand under her jumper to capture a taught nipple between his finger and thumb, rolling it coaxingly to feverish arousal.

She moaned low in her throat with the sizzling excitement of the moment and moved her ungloved hand up his chest and over his broad shoulder and around his neck to play with the softness of the hair at his nape.

Lucas released her mouth to taste her neck, trailing hot kisses along her throat. She threw her head back, allowing him access as he shifted even closer, quickly shoving her jumper aside to capture an already hard nipple between his lips, suckling urgently.

This was his fantasy come true. Lucas lapped lovingly and moulded her perky breasts in his hands, cupping the weight of them as they fit perfectly into his palms as he knew they would.

While the hot, almost savage roughness of his mouth wreaked havoc on her other breast, Saffron opened her eyes in discomfort, and for some reason focused on a red plastic-handled spatula hanging on the wall. Red. Red lipstick. The snake! He'd been kissing the blonde before he'd been kissing her!

"Stop!" she cried, and with arms feeling like overcooked noodles she pushed at his broad shoulders. The dragging of his mouth from her tender breasts was almost her undoing, but she pushed hard and he finally released her.

They were both breathing heavily, and she saw his naked desire before he blinked and turned violently away from her, raking an unsteady hand through his hair as he strode out of the kitchen.

What the hell was that? Saffron asked herself as she looked down to see her jumper all askew. She put a hand to her lips, feeling them throb against her fingertips. Oh God. She could feel that same throb pulsating at the apex of her thighs. It had been a long time since she'd ever felt that feeling, and she burned for more.

For a moment she pressed the heel of her hand between her legs, hoping to relieve the pressure, but it didn't work. She pulled off the other rubber glove and ran cold water over her wrists. She felt sick. She felt excited. She felt scared. She didn't know what the hell she felt. This was Lucas, for God's sake.

Switching off the kitchen lights, she went into the other room. It was dark. Lucas stood stiffly by the opened front door with a hand on the heavy ornate door handle.

"I'm sorry about that," he apologised tightly as she attempted to move pass him.

If anything, his coldness ignited her temper. She stopped, turned and slapped him hard across the face.

"Don't you ever do that to me again." With her head held high, she swept out the door and marched down the street towards her building.

It was only ten minutes away, but still she felt lonely on the dark and deserted street. Lucas usually walked her home. The chilly evening air was making her shiver. She stomped hard on the ground. She reached her building, closed the glass lobby door and attempted to lift a hand to wave to Lucas as she'd done a million times before. He was there, under the lamppost, the orange glow highlighting his grimness. He didn't smile. She didn't wave. Her heart broke as she realized that their relationship would never be the same.

❧❧❧❧❧

Lucas let himself into his penthouse apartment, and for once he didn't appreciate the restful interior of creams and greens a top designer had worked painstakingly to create to his exacting tastes. He walked over to the floor-to-ceiling windows, not noticing the sweeping views of the sprawling city below, or the ghostly sphere of St. Barnabos Cathedral. He didn't even see the glassy darkness of the Beeston Canal as it meandered like a graceful snake in the stillness. With a flick of his wrist he snapped the mahogany blinds shut.

Walking over to his drinks cabinet, he poured himself a healthy measure of whisky and knocked it back, feeling it scorch his throat with painful satisfaction.

He couldn't believe what they'd done. What he'd done. Usually he was able to control his baser instincts around her, but not tonight. Oh no. Tonight he'd gone off the rails.

He'd avoided touching her as usual, and there wasn't anything remotely erotic about the way she had licked her finger and cleaned his face as if rubbing away the signs of another woman was an everyday occurrence.

For a split second, as her brown eyes had teasingly captured his, he thought that maybe, just maybe, she knew how he felt and that she wanted the platonic barriers, which kept their relationship clean, solid, and pure, to be breached.

He remembered feeling his blood thicken, a strange heat surging through his veins, and he'd wanted to flatten her against the sofa, sink his body into hers and take her so hard and fast she'd forget her own name. He'd had to bite his tongue hard to stop his hands from reaching for her.

Lucas poured himself another whisky and walked over to his favourite chair, kicking off his shoes along the way. Flinging himself down, he closed his eyes. Bloody hell, what a night! He could still taste her, smell her, and feel the soft silkiness of her smooth skin. God, what a mess! He dragged a not-so-steady hand through his dark hair.

She'd never forgive him, he thought. Saffron was loyal to the point of bloody stupidity. And even now, she was probably on the phone, confessing all to that prat of a boyfriend in Jamaica.

Frustrated and angry, Lucas stormed into his luxurious bathroom of black and grey mosaic tiles, stripped and stepped into the shower stall, bracing himself as he abruptly turned off the mixer. Cold water poured like a thousand sharp needles over his heated body.

There was nothing left for him to do but put his heart in her hands and confess all. If she trampled on it and threw it back in his face, well, at least he could then get on with his life. What was the point of loving someone who was in love with someone else?

But without her to warm his soul he'd probably become a cold, unfeeling bastard like the man he was supposed to call father.

Knowing how hard the next few minutes were going to be, he stepped out of the shower, roughly towelled himself and wrapping the towel around his waist, strode into his bedroom. With a loaded sigh, he reached for the phone.

ಹಿ-ಆ-ಶಿ-ಆ

Saffron was up to her neck in scented foam. In her anger, she'd poured the whole 180-pound bottle of designer bubbles into the bath water.

Blowing the pungent suds away from her nose, she leaned back and closed her eyes. What happened earlier tonight filled her with burning shame. She'd never felt like that before, and with Lucas of all people! Roderick's kisses had always been, well, pleasant. But tonight she'd experienced a scary kind of pleasure. It was so intense, so hot, so deliciously wicked, she'd been completely engulfed by it. Even now her nipples tingled at the memory.

How could she ever face Lucas again? And what on earth was she going to say to Roderick? She couldn't phone him tonight, knowing she'd been messing around with another man. And enjoying it. He'd hear the guilt in her voice. No, she wouldn't ring him.

Saffron had always known that Lucas had a dark side, but for him to use her and sacrifice their friendship just because he was horny made her blood boil.

How dare he treat her that way. Just because the tramp he'd really wanted had left without him tonight, he thought he could finish the evening off with her. The bastard, she seethed. She, Saffron Ayeisha Noble, was not going to be a substitute for any man.

Getting up so suddenly that water splashed onto the tiled floor, she reached for a towel and wrapped it around her body, securing it under her arms as she stomped into her bedroom, flung herself onto the bed and snatched up the phone.

⊱❀⊰

"I think someone is trying to tell you something, lass," noted Mairead, Saffron's feisty Scottish shop assistant, speaking in the rhythmic Gaelic voice Saffron loved so much.

Saffron shrugged as she accepted and signed for another cottage-styled bouquet of tall purple and gold flowers. "Yeah, well, I should really send them all back." They'd been coming on the hour since lunch time.

"Tut tut, you young people," Mairead said, shaking her head. "A slight tiff and you throw in the towel. Come here," she ordered with a wave of her arm. Saffron followed her five foot assistant across the room, smiling as sunlight caught the bright redness of her frizzy hair, making it look like the flaming beacon of the Olympic torch.

Mairead stopped by a heavy crystal vase filled with tall, thick stemmed flowers with heads of hundreds of tiny, bell-shaped, lilac-coloured petals. She touched a petal with her brown, freckled hands. "These here are hyacinths. I call it the sorry flower. It's what my Jimmy always sends me when he's been at the pub too long," she whispered with a wink. "And this," she said, pointing to the basket Saffron had just put down on a table, "this wee basket is filled with peonies and irises. Loose translation? Forgiveness and friendship. Put the two of them together and what does it mean?" A heavily pencilled eyebrow rose as she looked at Saffron with searching expectation.

Saffron's eyes shimmered with tears, a lump tightening her throat.

"Oh lass, don't you go a-crying now," Mairead soothed. "He's telling you sorry for whatever he's done and he's begging for forgiveness. It's only a real man who can do that, lass. Not a red rose man this." She went on with obvious approval. "He's deeper, stronger, a man who knows what he's about. A real keeper. This one has passion in his soul, lass. Do I know who it is?" Mairead asked eagerly.

"Lucas," Saffron admitted reluctantly. She just couldn't equate Lucas and passion in the same sentence.

"Ahh," Mairead said, a soft glimmer of understanding coming into her eyes. "That bouquet you're holding has purple and golden loosestrife in it. They're peace offering flowers. It's the colour as well as the flower which sends the message," she explained. "Come on now, cheer up, lass, and let's get back to work," Mairead added as a young couple came in holding hands.

Just before closing, a uniformed delivery man brought in a small blue box marked 'fragile' written in tiny gold letters all over it.

Saffron put it on the counter, pushing a basket of faux ivory Chinese charms out of the way before ringing through the last sale of the day. Then she walked over to the door, turned the sign over to 'closed' before walking back to the counter to stand and stare at the box.

"Well open it, lass," Mairead encouraged excitedly. "I'm about to go home, and this is all the excitement I'm gonna get for tonight! My Jimmy is out on a fishing trip this weekend."

With a laugh, Saffron opened the package to find a tiny porcelain fairy holding a white flower up to the sky as though in offering.

"It's beautiful." She traced a finger along the delicate three-inch figurine.

"Aye, that it is," said Mairead.

"What kind of flower is she holding?" Saffron asked the expert beside her.

Mairead squinted down at it. "It looks like a weed," she said.

"Weed!"

18

"Bindweed, lass, not like the regular roadside weed. It means something really important. I'll nip to the bookshop and get a book. I need to know. Oh, this is exciting, lass, very exciting!"

Saffron smiled weakly as she watched the pint-sized, amble-bodied Mairead rush out of the shop and down the stairs with the dexterity of an athlete.

The fairy was indeed exquisitely made. Again a lump formed in Saffron's throat. She missed Lucas. She was still mad at him, but she missed him. It wasn't like they saw each other every day. She felt as though she'd lost her best friend. In a way, she had, and it upset her.

❧❧❧❧

Lucas stood in the doorway of The Mother Lode, feeling unsure of his next move. Knowing Saffron's temper, he hoped the meanings of his flowers had softened her after three days of silence. He'd tried to ring her that night but she'd been on the phone, talking to the boyfriend, no doubt.

She hadn't seen him yet and was busy pouring over a thick book on the counter. Mairead was ringing up the till.

"I've found it, Mairead! Look here, it means, and I quote, 'I abase myself and ask for your forgiveness'. Oh Mairead!" Saffron fought to control her tears, and for a second, allowed Mairead to comfort her.

A nudge on her shoulder made her look at her assistant who, in turn, nodded towards Lucas standing in shadow in the doorway.

"I'll just go finish this in the back room." Mairead quickly gathered up the receipts, leaving an uneasy silence behind.

Lucas had never felt so awkward in his life. He always knew what he was about, and only being around Saffron made him feel like an unsure kid.

Saffron had only seen Lucas in a suit once before and that had been the day he signed the lease for the coffee bar. Today, he seemed taller, his shoulders wider. The suit was charcoal and worn with a mint green shirt and a green and gold striped tie. He took her breath away.

He moved towards her and Saffron forced herself to breathe. Cassidy was right, she thought: he did have the most unusual eyes. A tawny gold that reminded her of a brilliant Jamaican day at the beach. His eyelashes were black, thick and long. Strange how she'd never noticed them before either.

"Do you?" he said, clearing his throat. "Do you forgive me, I mean?"

His voice sounded deeper, seeming to flow over and all around her. It was comforting.

"I've never received flowers before," Saffron hedged. "Thank you." The silence was long, deep and awkward. She could hear Mairead talking to herself in the back room.

"I'm glad to be the first," Lucas responded.

Saffron's eyes narrowed as she remembered that she was supposed to be mad at him and not impressed by his meaningful flowers and beautiful mouth.

"How about we go get something to eat and talk about what happened," Lucas suggested.

"Oh, you mean the other night when you all but mauled me!"

Lucas paled. "I didn't maul you," he said stiffly.

"So what do you call this?" Saffron opened her amber silk shirt to show him the love bite.

He looked at it, his eyes flashing rich gold as he lifted his eyes to capture hers. She was mesmerised but took refuge behind her anger.

"That and more!" she shouted.

"More?"

"Never mind that. What got into you?" she asked.

"Look, I have something I need to say. I–."

Mairead walked in, bag in hand. "I'll be seeing you on Monday, lass. Good night, young Lucas. Nice flowers."

"Good night, Mairead," they both said in unison.

"And before you tell me how sorry you are," Saffron uttered, turning back to Lucas, "let me assure you, I don't want to hear it! But if you ever use me the way you did, I swear, Lucas, you will live to regret it!"

Lucas stared at her; she was nothing if not magnificent in her anger, breasts heaving and ponytail flying. He smiled.

"And you can wipe that smirk of your face! I'm bloody angry!" Saffron slapped her hands on the counter and leaned towards him. "But to treat me, Lucas, as just another one of your women, it hurt. You used me because I was there." She folded her arms across her breasts. "Admit it, and we can both forget the incident and get back to how we were." She looked him square in the eyes. "You know what else hurts me, Lucas?" she began again. "You really want to know? I bet you don't even remember her name! You—."

"Tallulah," he answered smoothly, interrupting her tirade.

"What?"

"Her name is Tallulah, and I'm taking her out next week."

Saffron couldn't believe the rage she felt upon hearing that piece of information. Not two nights ago he forgot all about his Tallulah and was having it on with her. The cad! And what kind of name was Tallulah anyway?

"Well good! Good for you." She plastered a smile on her face. She was going to be happy for him if it killed her. "You and I have been friends too long to end because you were feeling horny for some ten-pence slapper!"

His eyebrows rose at her statement. It was so unlike her. "She's not a slapper, Saffron."

"Whatever," Saffron replied with a flick of her wrist. "I love Roderick and I want to marry him."

Her words cut. She loved Roderick. Hell, he knew that all along, but to hear her say it with such passion and conviction slaughtered him. A man has his pride after all.

He caught her hand, trying to ignore the zing that flew up his arm when their fingers touched. "I don't know what happened," he began, "you were there, we were shouting and I forgot who I was with for a moment." She flinched. Good, he thought. "You are my best friend and I missed you. I'm sorry," he said

She looked at their entwined fingers. His pale, hers golden. Milk and honey, it was oddly comforting.

"I missed you, too." Saffron leaned over the counter and kissed him on the cheek. "Thanks for the fairy. How come you know so much about flowers anyway?"

"My mother," Lucas admitted, his handsome face hardening. And again she wondered what Lucas was hiding since he never talked about his family.

"Oh, that's nice. Mairead had to go out and buy me a flower meaning book. She got stuck on those purple thingies over there." They laughed easily together, knowing Saffron didn't have a clue when it came to the names, much less the meaning, of flowers. She had contracted an agency to look after the plants in her flat.

"Come on. Let's go get something to eat," Lucas said, looking at his watch.

"I can't. I've got too much to do here," she explained.

"Can I help or anything?" he asked, looking around. Saffron followed his gaze and saw him peering out the shop window at the throngs of late shoppers still milling around.

"You're a good man, Lucas James Bridgwater."

He stiffened, swung around to face her with a hard frown and released her hand. "Don't call me that!" he snarled.

"Sorry, but it is your name. Why so defensive?"

"Let's leave it, okay," he replied, trying to sound calm. "Meet me at the corner at the regular time in the morning, and we'll go for a jog down by Victoria Embankment."

He walked out quickly before she could confirm his plans or ask about his suit.

Chapter Two

I had been a busy two days, what with new stock coming in from Tunisia to record, price and then display in the already overcrowded shop. With a huge yawn, Saffron changed into her white hooded towelling robe and breathed a sigh of heavenly relief. She intended to spend the rest of the evening taking a bath, reading a thriller and not thinking about Lucas's mouth.

She was about to run her bath when the doorbell rang. The last thing she wanted tonight was company, but she changed her mind when she looked through the peephole and saw Cassidy on the other side.

"Hey, come in," Saffron said. "If it was anybody else, I'd have pretended to be out." She led the way into her exotic-looking living room, filled with brightly coloured Moroccan cushions, throws and an abundance of silver and glass candle-holders and ornaments. One wall was painted in a deep red and boasted an array of round mirrors. Another was burnt orange and another was brown. The place was set off beautifully by the plush white carpet.

"Why, it's not even half past eight," Cassidy said, looking at her watch and toeing off her worn trainers at the same time.

"I know, but it's been a long week," Saffron replied.

"Well, sorry to say this, but tomorrow is Saturday, your busiest day."

"You are a real chum, aren't you, for that reminder," Saffron teased. "Go help yourself in the kitchen, while I put something on."

She pulled on a pair of baggy pink-striped pyjamas she'd picked up in North Africa and paired it with a skinny pink vest.

"That's disgusting!" Saffron said, walking into the kitchen sometime later and catching Cassidy spoon a mouthful of cold baked beans straight from the can into her mouth. "The microwave is right there!"

Cassidy waved the spoon in the air. "I was hungry."

"I'll put the kettle on. Put that in the bin and I'll do some toast. Go put your feet up or something. You look done in." Saffron got the bread out and put several slices in the toaster.

Cassidy dropped the almost empty can in the rubbish bin with a thud. She moved around Saffron to wash her hands. "Then you can tell me all about that love bite on your neck as I certainly don't see any signs of Roderick about," she stated slyly as she left the kitchen.

Saffron's hand flew to the love bite just below her left collar bone. It was the only one visible. She had a scattering of them across her breasts. What was she going to say? I've got a boyfriend but couldn't keep my hands off Lucas? Lucas of all people.

The toast popped out, making her jump.

With a tray laden with a pot of tea, hot toast dripping with butter and two generous slices of raspberry cheesecake, Saffron carefully put the tray down on the table. Cassidy had her eyes closed.

"Are you asleep, Cass?" Saffron whispered.

"No, just closing my eyes for a minute."

"At work tonight, are you?"

"Yep." Cassidy rubbed her eyes then reached for a slice of toast, biting into it with a moan of ecstasy.

"Are you getting enough sleep? Because you don't look like you are," Saffron said.

"I get my eight hours, just not altogether." Cassidy poured cups of tea for both of them and turned to face her friend. "So are you going to tell me about it?" she asked, referring to the love bite.

Saffron took a deep breath and replied, "Lucas did it."

"Lucas?" Cassidy's eyes widened incredulously. "As in our hunky friend with the great body and fabulous eyes, Lucas?"

"Lucas is not hunky, he's just, well, Lucas."

"That's because you've never really looked at him. He's gorgeous."

"Yeah well, gorgeous or not, he had no right to attack me."

"He attacked you?!" Cassidy all but yelled.

"Not attack, in that way. What I mean to say is," Saffron tried again clumsily. How could she explain it to her friend when she couldn't even explain it to herself? "We were fighting, and I told him he should have gone with that blonde girl who was pawing all over him. He got mad, things were said and the next thing I knew, we were kissing."

"Wow, you slept with Lucas," Cassidy said, amazed but not really surprised. The chemistry between Lucas and Saffron had always been explosive.

"Lord no, I stopped it. There was no way I was going to replace that tramp he was with earlier."

"And that's the only reason?" Cassidy inquired.

"I like the way he kisses, okay. It took me a moment or two to get myself together, but it will never happen again!"

"So what did you say to him?"

"Nothing," Saffron said, sitting up and dusting crumbs from her pyjamas. "But enough about me. What's going on in your life apart from you working yourself to death?"

"I'm off to Leicester tomorrow night," Cassidy replied.

"Why? To see that investigator I suppose." It wasn't that Saffron didn't want Cassidy to find her son; it was just her friend's way of doing things that she didn't approve of. Cassidy wouldn't let her help in any way. And that hurt.

Cassidy nodded. "I need to pay him and start the arrangements for his trip to Goa."

"No way am I letting you give that man any more money! Wasn't it only last week or so you gave him a couple hundred? Are you sure he's not planning a holiday trip to Goa at your expense? And how much does he charge anyway?" Saffron asked.

Cassidy quoted a figure.

"My God! No wonder you're working two jobs. Let me help you," Saffron said, raising a hand to stop Cassidy from interrupting. "I know you won't take the cash, but I have friends, Cass. Influential friends. Let me ask them to make some enquiries before you give away anymore money. Please," she begged.

Cassidy took a deep breath. It was hard for her to rely on anyone. People always let her down. She didn't want her friendship with Saffron to suffer because of disappointment. That's why she'd never asked anything of her in all these years. She needed her friendship.

The phone ringing in the bedroom made Saffron get up. It was Roderick. He'd reversed the charges. Saffron hung up minutes later, making a mental note to go to the bank to get some money for him. His mother needed medication desperately.

Back in the living room, Saffron found Cassidy curled up fast asleep. With a tender look, she covered her friend with a heavy woollen throw. Cassidy would be mad that she didn't wake her up, but she'd deal with that in the morning. Right now, Saffron knew her friend needed a good night's sleep.

❧❧❧❧

It was early afternoon, and Saffron reluctantly got out of the bath before Lucas got home. This was her eighth day here, and as pleasant as his flat was, she missed indulging in long leisurely baths and pampering herself with expensive lotions and oils. Mairead was closing the shop for her today.

Saffron patted herself dry with a large fluffy navy blue towel before pouring a generous amount of scented body oil into her palm, rubbing her hands together and then rubbing it into her skin, starting at her toes, sweeping up her thighs and over her hips, before repeating the process on her upper body. Then, rinsing off the hard cucumber face mask in cold water, she moisturised her face and neck, swept shimmering body powder over herself and then slipped on a pair of pink lacy low-cut panties with a matching spaghetti strap top.

She felt fantastic and, for once, the annoyance of having her flat flooded by the one above hers was forgotten. Three weeks, the insurance company had said, it would take before her flat was liveable again.

She was walking to her bedroom and singing softly to herself when the front door opened. In mid stride Saffron froze.

Lucas stood transfixed in the doorway, his dark eyes flashing as they raked over her body, up her long brown legs, stopping a moment at the apex before roaming hungrily over her breasts and up her neck until their eyes met. Saffron couldn't breathe.

"Lucas?" she whispered. She didn't understand why she was saying his name when she should have been running for cover. This was just the sort of situation she had wanted to avoid. She didn't want to feel the hot sensual heat that was spreading throughout her body like a wave of scorching molten lava. She didn't want to feel the heaviness in her aroused breasts, the peaking of her nipples nor the drowsy breathlessness that made her feel wanton, reckless and powerfully female.

Lucas kicked the door shut and, with his eyes keeping her frozen in place, walked casually towards her, loosening his colourful tie and dropping it to the thick carpet. Saffron watched, transfixed, as he unbuttoned the top button of his shirt with determined fingers.

He finally stood in front of her so close she could feel his warm breath fanning her face. She could smell peppermint. His eyes were smoky, so black she could see her own desire reflected in the dark depths. This was everything she wanted and everything she did not.

He reached out, running his fingers with feathery light circles on her smooth shoulder, making her tremble inside.

"Don't." Her lips formed the word, but her eyes pleaded with him to do something more.

"Don't, Saffron?" His beautiful voice was deep, thick with need and snaking around her, roping her in. He ran a finger along her collar bone, dipping into the tiny vee at the centre, playing there a moment before slowly moving to the other side. "Don't do this, Saffron?" he asked sensually, a small smile playing around his mouth. "Or this?" He put his tongue to her ear, leisurely swirling around the delicate shell and trailing soft tiny kisses down her throat.

He finally touched her mouth with his. She wasn't prepared for the gentleness of his kiss, the whispering caress as he moved his lips back and forth, back and forth over hers. She leaned forward, wanting to increase the pressure. He chuckled low in his throat.

"Bastard," she muttered, reaching her eager hands into his thick black hair, trying eagerly to capture his mouth.

"I'll give you what you want, honey. Anything you want," he promised, pressing against her lips and swooping his mouth down hard on hers. She loved it.

Somehow they were on the sofa, the coolness of the leather distracting her briefly but soon forgotten. Lucas whipped her top over her head and captured a plump brown nipple in his mouth. She moaned as the pulsating suckle of his hot mouth sent wave upon wave of sexual heat down to her core. She snatched handfuls of his silky dark hair, pulling him to her mouth to kiss him deeply. He moved over her body, his legs sliding between hers, making her feel that part of him that promised to give her all she desired.

He was so hard. She lifted her hips as he tried in vain to ease the mounting pressure that was building inside her. With impatient fingers she pulled at his shirt, and he hauled it over his head, throwing it to the floor and almost frantically unsnapping his trousers before settling back into her arms, feverishly kissing her eyes, her ears and her throat.

He moved lower, gently nipping her stomach, swirling his hot tongue in her belly button before moving even lower. She stilled. His dark eyes locked with hers, and with a devilish smile he kissed her in that place she had never been kissed before.

"Lucas," she gasped in pleasure. He had to hold her writhing body steady while he loved her through the pink lace.

"Lucas?" she sobbed, reaching down and pulling him up by the hair to kiss him again and again while his fingers moved her panties aside to play within her delicate folds.

Somewhere just above them a phone was ringing. They both paused, but with a heated look Lucas continued to play with her body. The phone stopped but began again almost immediately.

With a heavy sigh, Lucas gently nipped her nipples before reluctantly reaching over her head to pick up the phone.

"This had better be good," he drawled huskily into the mouthpiece.

Saffron was revelling in a haze of heightened arousal and the throbbing promise of his erection between her legs when the sound of a hysterical female voice at the other end of the phone abruptly cut through her sensual fog.

"Yes, she's here." Lucas covered the mouthpiece and whispered with a trace of annoyance, "Tell her you're about to go out or something."

Saffron listened lazily then sat up, dislodging Lucas from her side, making him fall to the floor with a hard thud.

"She did what!" Saffron exclaimed over the phone, reaching for a cushion. Lucas watched with growing dismay, knowing the moment was now lost forever, as she covered her chest from him. He got up and refastened his trousers before walking painfully to the bathroom.

Saffron finished the call just as Lucas came out.

"I've got to go," she said, looking everywhere but at him.

"Don't think that what we just did didn't take place, Saffron," he assured her with supreme arrogance. "We'll talk about it later." For good measure, he came over and gave her a searing kiss and fondled her breasts. "You'd better get dressed," he suggested with a rakish smile, watching with satisfaction as her eyes slowly cleared of the passion he could so easily arouse.

Saffron closed the door to Lucas's flat and leaned against it. She was alone, she noticed with relief, and kicked off her boots, unwound her tan and pink-striped cashmere scarf and went to make herself a cup of tea.

She put water in the kettle, plugged it in and looked out the small kitchen window at the gloomy night sky. There wasn't a star in sight.

Cassidy had followed an Asian boy home today, forced her way into his house and accused his family of kidnapping. The boy's family had been about to phone the police when Cassidy collapsed and told the boy's mother her story. Then they called Saffron.

It had been a long and emotional evening for Saffron: picking Cassidy up, apologising profusely to the family and then taking her home. Cassidy didn't want to stay with her at Lucas's place, so Saffron had seen her settled at her own bed-sit in Radford before leaving her.

Saffron made the tea and went into the living room, sitting on Lucas's high-tech recliner to relax before turning the TV on. She found the remote and put the TV on mute.

Something needed to be done about Cassidy, Saffron thought, knitting her eyebrows. The girl was definitely obsessed and becoming increasingly unstable. She had spent too many years looking at every little brown skinned boy with grey eyes in the street. She needed closure before she did something really stupid.

Taking a sip of the tea, Saffron noticed the cushions on the sofa not neatly aligned as Lucas liked them to be. They were flattened and askew, and she couldn't help remembering the last time she'd been on the sofa.

She didn't understand what was going on between her and Lucas. They were best friends. Best friends didn't sleep with each other and remain best friends for long, and she didn't want to lose him. She couldn't even begin to imagine him not being on the other end of the phone line or running beside her down by the Embankment. But this sudden sexual attraction she was feeling for him didn't feel right. Yet every time he was near her lately, she noticed something new and sexually exciting about him.

Could she and Lucas become lovers and still remain as close as they are now? Should they even try? Did she love him? Only as a friend, she was sure. Did he love her? No, Lucas loved women, but only in bed. Aside from her, he didn't keep female friends. And those he did sleep with lasted less than a few weeks. Why would he want to jeopardise what they have for a quick bout of hot sex? Did he see her as just another woman to sleep with?

Saffron quickly gulped down the rest of the tea, scorching her tongue in the process, and went to the bathroom to have a shower. She needed to talk to him.

Then, changing into a clean pair of black designer jeans, a long black chunky jumper and a pair of trainers, she let herself out.

It was cold and she rubbed her hands together as she walked quickly down to the coffee bar. The front door was already locked and the entrance lights switched off. Jogging around to the side entrance, Saffron opened the door with her key. The place was in darkness. Walking through the kitchen, she made her way to the front, her trainers silent against the shiny tiles.

"Lu–," she started and then stopped, stunned. Lucas and Tallulah were kissing passionately. He wasn't even pulling away, Saffron noticed stricken. He was groaning.

Gutted, Saffron stood transfixed for a millisecond then fled as soundlessly as she had arrived. Within the hour, she was back at her own flat. She wouldn't cry, she told herself, as she violently shoved the mop into the mop bucket, roughly wrung it out and mopped the floor. She didn't mind that a cleaning agency was due to come in the next day to do it anyway. Her flat was still a mess, but at least the sodden carpet had been removed.

She'd had a lucky escape, she convinced herself as she splashed water about. Just thinking about him with that tart, kissing and moaning, was enough to make her want to throw things.

Lucas was highly sexed. Saffron had seen the women come and go in and out of his life as if they were on a conveyor belt. God, she was stupid, she thought.

Never again, she told herself savagely, stabbing the mop in the bucket, not bothering to wring it out.

A knock at the door startled her, causing her to drop the mop.

"Open up, Saff, it's me. I don't have my key," Lucas called through the door.

For a brief moment Saffron froze and then, with a shrewd smile, she picked up her mobile phone and tiptoed quietly to the door, unlatching it before moving stealthily away.

"Saffron, it's me. It's time for that talk, sweetheart."

Hypocrite, she thought meanly. "It's open," she called before turning her back to the door.

"Yes, Roderick," she giggled breathlessly into her mobile. "I know." She sneaked a peak at Lucas over her shoulder. He stood, frozen, by the door, his eyes narrow, cold and furious. He held a small posy of white flowers so tightly Saffron could see the whiteness of his knuckles. Where did he get flowers at this time of the night? she wondered.

"Yes, I love you too." Giggle. "You're so naughty. Bye, babe." She blew a kiss down the phone before finishing the fictitious call.

She turned, plastering a smile on her face. "Hi, Lucas, that was Roderick," she offered.

"Roderick," he snarled, stepping completely into the room and slamming the door behind him.

Saffron backed up as he came menacingly towards her. Her thighs met the table and she leaned back as he loomed over her.

"Ar...Are those for me?" she enquired sweetly, twisting slightly to look pointedly at the flowers he was strangling.

Lucas, briefly distracted, glanced down and with tight deliberation, he dropped the posy to place his hands on either side of the table, trapping Saffron between them.

"Did you tell him what you were doing today, Saffron?" He caught the back of her neck, forcing her to look into his fierce tawny gaze. "Did you tell him that only a few hours ago you were so hot and wet for me, you practically tore my clothes off, hmm? You want me, Saff. You can't deny it," he whispered cruelly, pushing his hand under her jumper to skim his palm over her nipples. "You didn't even remember him did you, Saff? When I did this to you." He massaged her breasts, and, using one hand, lifted her leg high as he pushed his hard thick member against her.

She closed her eyes, allowing herself to remember.

"I..." she mutterd. For a moment she was going to confess, but pulling herself together and pushing out of his reach, she moved around the table, putting the expanse of smoky glass between them.

"Lucas," she forced nonchalantly, "what can I say." She spread her arms out wide. "I was caught up in the moment. You were there and well–." She couldn't go on. If Lucas was a violent man she'd be dead right now. He was that angry. A single vein stood throbbing on his forehead; his eyes were flashing bloody murder and his lips thin, tight and bloodless.

She forced herself to shrug as though nothing mattered. That he didn't matter.

"It got out of hand, Lucas," she reasoned. "I'm sorry. I love Roderick. He'll be here within the month." She was lying.

She thought she saw a flash of pain but was probably mistaken. Lucas had no feelings when it came to women. He was a womanising swine, and she needed to remember that.

"You bitch!" Lucas swore, and with a casualness that belied his flushed angry face, walked out, closing the door with a soft click behind him.

Saffron collapsed against the table, but she was determined not to cry. This was for the best. Who needed Lucas? She had lots of friends.

As for Roderick, she swept up the phone again, stabbed his number into it and waited. She'd give him a month to come over, or it was finished. She was not going to give Lucas the satisfaction of being right about that too.

❧ ❧ ❧ ❧

Saffron glanced up at the clock, startled to realise it was so late. She was lucky there was a pub on the first floor of the shopping mall or she would have had to go searching for security to let her out of the building.

She hauled herself up from the stock room floor and shook her legs one by one, trying to get the circulation going again as she had been sitting in the cramped room for over an hour.

She'd only planned to do some accounts, but seeing a long lonely night ahead, she had started on the inventory of items just in from Turkey.

Switching off the lights and locking up, she made a mental note to stop at the chip shop and have a chicken kebab for dinner.

Taking the stairs down, she nervously watched a group of rowdy men. They all wore short-sleeved check shirts of various colours and all had gelled spiky hair as though in uniform. They were laughing and swearing loudly as they drank from almost empty pint glasses.

Saffron swore silently, as one of the men had seen her and was making his way towards her.

"Hey, it's an angel! Look lads, I've found me an angel. Where'd d'you come from, pretty face?" he asked, stopping at the bottom of the steps, his hands on both brass rails, blocking her in. She stayed a good five steps above him but said nothing.

"Hey, fellas!" he called to his friends, beckoning them over. "Who said I can't pull! Look at *vis vish* this one," he slurred. "She fell right from the sky." He laughed, his friends joining him and patting him on the back.

"Look, can I pass?" Saffron asked irritably.

"Only if you teach me to fly angel," he replied, swaying slowly as if being pulled by a magnet.

"Sorry, I left my wings at home tonight," Saffron answered tightly, hoping to see a security guard before this encounter escalated. She just wanted to get home.

"Ah, you ish no fun," the drunk sulked, pushing out his bottom lip.

"I'll bring my wings tomorrow night. How about that?"

He brightened. "You promise?"

"I promise, but only if you let me pass?" she coaxed hopefully.

"Ok." Sheepishly he put his hands in his pockets and moved away. "G'night, angel face."

"Good night." Saffron smiled, giving him a good-hearted wave as she turned to leave. He really was as non-threatening as a six-year-old.

She hadn't taken twenty steps before being caught in the middle of a group of loud pub crawlers. She'd never get home at this rate, she thought, as she fought her way through the drunken throng.

"Excuse me, excuse me," she said, pushing her way through.

"Oi, you!" Someone poked her in the back. She turned ready to do battle. Enough was enough. She was not going to be pawed and poked by a set of drunken yobs.

"Me?" she challenged, her dark eyes narrowing furiously.

"Yeah."

Saffron looked down at a busty blonde with fluffy platinum blonde hair, dark roots and bright red lipstick. Tallulah.

"I can see you. Remember me?" The blonde smiled drunkenly.

"Lucas's place, right?"

"As if you don't know." Tallulah arched an I-know-your-game kind of eyebrow. "I got me a new boyfriend now. He owns a fitness centre. No competition, darling, no competition," she slurred.

"That's nice." Where was she going with this? Saffron thought.

Tallulah glanced around, squinting into the semi-darkness then, grabbing Saffron's forearm, dragged her to one side.

"I need to confess something," Tallulah began in a slurring whisper, leaning forward. Saffron hoped the girl's large breasts weren't about to explode out of her skimpy sequined top. "You know what they say, confession is good for the soul and all that," Tallulah added with a wave of her hand.

Saffron smiled tightly.

"I know you fancy, Lucas," Tallulah continued. "So that night..."

"What night?" Saffron interrupted impatiently.

"That night you came back to Lucas's place."

Saffron stared at her blankly. "That night you saw me kissing him," she clarified impatiently, "wasn't one of my proudest moments, you see. But I saw you pass the side window and I just kinda flung myself at him and hung on."

"You saw me?" Not many things floored Saffron, but this certainly did.

Tallulah nodded. Tears welling up and escaping down her cheeks, taking half of her sky blue mascara with it.

"He gave me a proper dressing down. It was a stupid thing to do," she apologised.

"He wasn't kissing you back?" Saffron asked to be sure.

"He never kissed me period. I did all the kissing, behaving like a tramp."

Saffron had to smile at the word she herself had used on many occasions to describe Tallulah.

"He was gutted, you know," Tallulah added casually.

"No, I don't know."

"He went back to the café about an hour later, and I was outside talking to this bloke. So I peeped inside. He was flinging glasses and all sorts," Tallulah informed her, speaking in a strong Nottinghamshire accent that knocked of the last sounds of every word. "He was so angry. Way too emotional for a party girl like me. I don't do deep and emotional. But all's well that ends well, aint it. I met my Charlie that night," Tallulah added, beaming.

Tallulah was nothing if not resourceful, Saffron thought, admiring the girl's honesty. "Thanks, Tallulah." She gave her a small hug and turned to leave.

"You'll go after him, right?" Tallulah called after her. "I love a happy ending."

Saffron shrugged.

"You've got to go! Closure and all that," Tallulah added, noticing Saffron's indecision. Then she looked past Saffron and waved to a muscular guy with a shaved head and several thick gold chains hanging around his neck. "That's my Charlie," she gushed.

Saffron smiled at him.

"Look, I've got to go," Tallulah said, moving past then holding onto Saffron's arm for balance. "I may not be the brightest star in the sky, but Lucas only has eyes for you. Forget the battle, sweetheart. You'd already won the war and you didn't even know it." Tallulah laughed as she turned to rejoin her group, leaving Saffron standing in the middle of the shopping centre with a stunned expression on her face.

⇘⇘⇘

Standing slightly lopsided with two heavy white paper bags in each hand, Saffron stood facing the shiny black door of Lucas's flat. It was amazing, she thought, how this simple wooden object could divide her present and future so solidly.

Squaring her shoulders, she tapped on the door. She could hear the faint strains of a romantic orchestral masterpiece she couldn't name. She'd never known Lucas to listen to anything other than lively jazz. She tapped on the door again somewhat harder than she had intended.

It flew open and Lucas, bare chested and dishevelled, stood glaring down at her. Their eyes locked for a moment before his stormy gaze travelled down her body. By the time he looked into her eyes again, his cold mask was very much in place.

Unperturbed, Saffron lifted the two bags and prodded them against his chest.

"Chinese," she said, noticing his quizzical glance. She stepped past him into the flat to go directly to the kitchen.

Closing the door, Lucas tracked her to the kitchen. She was already getting his heavy oriental plates from the cupboard and setting them down on the table before opening a drawer to get the utensils out.

Putting the bags on the counter, he lodged himself against the door frame and folded his arms across his chest, waiting. His burnished gaze, intent and watchful.

"What are you doing here?" he eventually asked.

Saffron turned to look at him properly. His black hair was in need of a haircut again. It flopped with a slight wave onto his forehead.

She'd seen him dressed this way a thousand times: His chest bare and the worn grey tracksuit bottoms he favoured riding low on his narrow hips.

Her mouth dried, and pulling herself up to her full height, she forced herself to look him in the eye.

"I missed you," she admitted in a husky whisper, then licked her lips nervously.

"I'm sorry I acted the way I did and if you—" She stumbled. Her tongue felt as light as a slab of concrete. "If you still want me, I mean us, t-to you know, do something about this—" she petered out, waving her hands, as words failed her.

He said nothing, but moved his bare feet soundlessly across the cream floor tiles, took the knives and forks from her to set them down before turning to the bags, emptying them of the contents.

"Let's eat."

That's it? Saffron thought as she sat down abruptly. She admits that she wants him and all he wants to do is eat!

"Calm down," Lucas said.

"What, you can read minds now?" she challenged sarcastically, her dark eyes smouldering like black ash.

"I know you. We'll talk later."

"No, I want to talk now!" She watched him calmly spoon egg fried rice onto his plate and felt her temper rise.

Feeling her watching him, he put the spoon down with a deliberate clank and leaned back with his hands behind his head and looked at her. She was practically leaping with rage.

"You come here after what, a month or so and expect me to be jumping up and down with glee that you want me, Saffron?" he scoffed. "I'm sorry, sweetheart; you should know me by now."

His gaze flashed coldly into hers. His handsome face showed as much emotion as a Roman bust. Cold, bold, arrogant, and remote.

Saffron shivered. He'd moved on, she thought hopelessly. He doesn't want me.

"I thought we were friends," she said.

Lucas grimaced, his upper lip curling savagely, and rocked back on his chair. "We've moved beyond that, don't you think?" With quick movement he got up and strode into the living room, where he turned up the lights and switched off the CD player. Enough of the games, he thought, walking to the window to look out.

Saffron reluctantly followed at a slower place.

"Do you want me to leave?" she asked wearily.

"Where is lover boy?"

"You mean Roderick?" she answered nervously.

"Why, how many other poor sods have you got by the balls?" he asked.

Saffron stepped back as if struck. She couldn't deal with him like this. He swung round to face her, his gaze hot and accusing.

"It's over," she admitted reluctantly. "I gave him the month to come to England or that's it."

"You bitch," Lucas growled, stalking over to her and grabbing her shoulders to shake her roughly. "So he doesn't show and all of a sudden you want to be in my bed!" His mouth twisted with distaste. "I don't think so." He shook his head. "You should at least admit you were wrong, Saffron. All those years wasted on a man who didn't love you. Lock the door behind you," he called out before walking away and closing his bedroom door with an ominous thud.

Dumbfounded, Saffron stood staring at the closed door. With her shoulders slumped, she went to fetch her handbag from the kitchen before heading to the front door.

No, she thought, raising her chin, she was not going to just quietly go away. She had to convince him that she now knew what he had always known.

She walked to his bedroom, removing every scrap of clothing before entering.

It was dark, but she could see his outline beneath the white sheet.

"I told you to leave," he spoke coolly from his relaxed position against the headboard.

"I couldn't leave," she admitted, walking to the side of the bed, lifting the sheet and getting in before she lost her nerve.

She knelt beside him, her knees touching his hairy thigh as she picked up his hand and laid it on her small naked breast.

"It took me a long time. But I feel it," she admitted softly. "I really feel it." Her nipple peaked against his palm and, encouraged by his silence, she leaned in close. For the first time ever she initiated their kisses.

His lips remained cold and unresponsive as she softly ran her tongue against his mouth and then gently nipped at his bottom lip, moving over him to suck at it properly. Her erect nipples brushed across his chest, sending a tight coil of longing shooting to her genitals. She repeated the movement as she spread herself on top of him. Breasts to chest and thigh to thigh.

His hands came up and moulded the tight rounded globes of her bottom, grinding her into the heavy thickness of his arousal. He groaned deep in his throat and opened his mouth for her teasing tongue to enter. She kissed him long and hard, telling him all she was feeling with each sweep of her tongue.

Then, with a victorious chuckle, Lucas flipped her onto her back and took over. He was going to drive her out of her mind, he promised himself, as he moved down her soft silky body to suck on her waiting brown nipples. By the time he was finished making love to her tonight she was going to feel every bit as frustrated as he had always felt around her. She was going to be begging him to take her, and he would do it over and over again. By the time tomorrow came, Saffron would know who she wanted.

"No more Roderick," Lucas ordered, surging into her with a hard possessive thrust.

Saffron's hips rose to meet him. She gasped and he paused, holding himself above her, his body pulsating as he tried to remain still and not slam into her again and again.

"No more Roderick" he gritted savagely, his handsome face twisting with pain and pleasure. Beads of sweat dotted his forehead, and Saffron was vaguely aware of the supreme effort it was taking him to stop. His entire body was shaking. With a subtle cunningness that was all woman, Saffron wrapped her long legs high around his waist and locked them at the ankles, forcing him to sink deeper into her.

"Say it," he ordered, groaning. "Say it!"

"Only you," Saffron whispered. "Only you."

Lucas's eyes flashed a triumphant gold, and with an animalistic growl he gathered her close and made love to her with an urgency that left her sure that he'd wanted her for a very long time. He was everywhere. He consumed her. There was no other way to describe it. No part of her was left without the trail of his tongue, the graze of his teeth and the stroke of his touch.

❧❧❧❧

When they were done, Saffron lay with her head on Lucas's shoulder, one leg over both of his. Her fingers played idly with his black and wiry chest hair.

"What happens now?" she asked, sleepily content.

Shifting slightly, Lucas rose onto one elbow and leaned over her, liking what he saw. Her lips were swollen with his kisses, her golden skin dewy and glowing and her dark eyes soft and dreamy. He wanted to jump on the bed, howl and beat his chest.

"The boyfriend is history," he announced, expecting some sort of challenge from her. "I mean it. I don't share."

"Yes," she replied, on the very edge of sleep.

"You'll move in here, and for a time we'll see how it goes."

Her eyes flew open. "See how it goes?"

"Bad choice of words," he grimaced. "I don't do marriage. You know that."

"I wasn't aware that I was asking."

"You've been engaged to one man for what? Five years? Your wedding dress has been hanging in the wardrobe ever since," he jeered. "You want marriage, kids, a cat and a holiday home in Jamaica. I'll give you the last two. Forget the rest."

Saffron gasped. "Just who the bloody hell do you think you are! I wouldn't marry you anyway, Lucas! I've seen the way you treat women. I've been ashamed of my own sex always making it so easy for you." She flung herself off the bed and hauled the sheet off him and wrapped it haphazardly around herself, his magnificent nudity temporarily distracting her.

"I don't want anything from you. I was engaged to Roderick. I didn't even want this." She threw him a look of disgust.

Moving swiftly, Lucas swung her up into his arms, laid her on the bed, jerked the sheet off and lay on top of her before she could leave the room.

"Honey, you were gasping for it. But say his name again and you will live to regret it. I don't share," he warned darkly before stealing a quick kiss. "Ok," he sighed. "We'll get married."

"Stuff marriage," Saffron responded with a click of her tongue. "You're too uptight, stodgy and completely unbending most of the time! And now you've gone and ruined everything by having sex with me."

"I didn't have sex with myself, Saffron," he challenged, stiffening with offence at being called uptight.

"Sex has ruined it."

"Speak for yourself." Lucas ran a hand down her body and up again to mould a breast possessively. "This has been the longest foreplay ever. This has been coming for years." He tongued her nipple and she shifted.

"I won't sleep with you again, Lucas," Saffron stated harshly, willing her body not to respond to the not-so-gentle sucking of her erect nipple. She failed.

"You can and you will. Willingly," he replied with conviction. "Our relationship has changed; we've got the friendship thing down pat. Now it's time for the sex. Lots and lots of sex." He went on, nudging her legs apart to gently enter her. "Lots and lots of sex," he repeated with a triumphant laugh as he moved again, and she moved with him.

Chapter Three

$\mathcal{T}$he corridor on the floor of Saffron's apartment looked unfamiliarly long and narrow. Saffron had never needed to use the stairs in all the years she'd been living in the building.

Rounding a corner, she stopped suddenly. A man was lying on the floor, his head cushioned by a black flight bag. She stepped back and peeped over at him from behind a large green cheese plant. The man was actually lying against her door.

Her heart hammering against her rib cage, Saffron bit her lip anxiously, wondering what to do. Never had she felt so vulnerable and alone. Making a quick decision to knock on the nearest door, she glanced again at the man for identification purposes, noticing his name brand boots, dark jeans and baggy wheat-coloured jumper. A blue baseball cap was pulled down on his head. She recognised the brightly coloured Air Jamaica baggage tags hanging from the bag. Roderick? Oh my God, she thought. It was Roderick!

She must have made a noise, as his head snapped up and he looked straight at her. He looked completely different, Saffron thought. His face was narrower with sharp angles and heavy eyelids. She'd expected him to look a bit more rugged, more mannish; however, his face was as smooth as it had been when they were teenagers, and his eyebrows looked trimmed and neatly shaped.

Saffron moved forward, watching nervously as he stood and held out his arms. The smile playing at the corner of his mouth was pure Roderick, a flash of perfect white teeth.

Saffron found herself wrapped in an awkward embrace. He kissed her cheek before quickly stepping back to look her over.

"Where you been, girl? I've been here all night," he said. The light conversational tone belied the inquisitive narrowing of his eyes.

"I'm sorry. I was out with friends, my girlfriends," she mumbled guiltily. She couldn't look at him. She dug in her bag instead for her keys. "I wasn't expecting you."

"Woman, you gave mi a month to get mi backside up here or we done. Dat's what you said. So here me is." With that he picked up his bags and stepped past her into her flat.

Roderick dropped his bags in the centre of the room and looked around.

"I'm glad you came," Saffron said, wrapping her arms around his lean waist. He was really skinny beneath the baggy clothes, and he was shorter than she remembered. Their eyes were level. Roderick dipped his head to plant a kiss on her jaw.

Over the years, Saffron had imagined that their reunion would be many things: passionate kisses, flowers and tears inside the North Terminal at Gatwick Airport. But this was more like the meeting of two strangers on a blind date.

"You smell kind of funny," Roderick said. Mortified, Saffron practically leapt out of his embrace and stepped away.

"Sorry. As I said, I was out," she said, now awkwardly aware of the smell of sex clinging to her skin. "You'll need to make yourself at home because I need to shower and go and open the shop." She walked backwards down the narrow hall, desperately wanting to distance herself so she could think. "You're probably dying to get some sleep anyway," she babbled. "Use my bed and we'll sort something out when I get back." She then fled to her room, locking the door and leaning against it with a heavy sigh.

Showering quickly, Saffron refused to think about anything other than getting herself to the shop and planting herself there. She dried herself and brushed her teeth before pulling on a pair of jeans and a jumper. Normally she'd spend a few minutes choosing her clothes and at least putting on some lipstick, but now she just wanted to leave. She was glad to see Roderick. She really was, she tried to convince herself. She only wished he'd been here twenty-four hours ago. A lot could happen in twenty-four hours.

Sighing heavily she sat on the edge of her bed to pull on her long, black leather boots with a row of silver buckles down the sides and tucked her jeans into them. Taking a deep breath, she squared her shoulders and reached for the bedroom door.

῾῾῾῾῾

With a heavy heart, Saffron climbed the stairwell for the second time that day. The lift was still out of order. She was tired, hungry and had dearly wished for the shop to be busy, but instead it was the quietest Saturday in a long time, with only a trickle of customers, and most of them were just browsing. She had too much time to think.

Sitting on the bottom stair between the fourth and fifth floors, Saffron decided to phone Lucas. He'd already rung twice today, and she'd fobbed him off with the excuse of being busy. His voice had sounded deeply sexy, with a hint of the lust of a satisfied lover who intended to come back for more. She'd run scared.

She had to tell him Roderick was here and ask for some time to figure out what to do. He'd be mad with her again for asking him to wait, and after last night who could blame him? But Roderick was here now. A week past her ultimatum, but he was here. She had to give it a go after waiting for him all these years.

If only he'd come when she'd told him to, then she would not have spent the night with Lucas. Saffron groaned in despair. She didn't know what to do.

Knowing she'd have to eventually phone Lucas and at least arrange to meet him somewhere, Saffron reluctantly used the voice dial, said his name into her sleek, trendy mobile phone and was enormously relieved when her phone beeped the no signal tone. She would ring him later and arrange to meet him tomorrow.

Shoving the phone into her large leather handbag, she got up, dusted off her bum and climbed the stairs, telling herself over and over that she was glad Roderick was here.

❦⋅❦⋅❦⋅❦

Having left her keys, Saffron knocked on the door to her flat to be let in. She stood in shock when a stranger opened it a short while later.

"May I help you?" the tall white man asked in a soft and cultured voice. He was intensely good-looking. "Are you here for someone?" he asked, raising a dark blonde eyebrow.

"This is my house," Saffron challenged, lifting her chin. What the hell was going on? And who the hell was this? she thought, getting angry.

The man rocked back on his heels to look her over. His dark stare of assessment travelled down then swiftly up her body before he stepped back giving her just enough space to pass.

"Roderick?" Saffron called, walking into the living room. "No, leave the door open," she told the stranger as he was about to close it.

He shot her a cold stare and she shivered.

"Roderick!" Saffron called out a second time, slightly panicked. She didn't like the way the stranger was watching her.

Roderick sauntered out of the bathroom with her peach-coloured hand towel wrapped around his waist. He was barely decent and had obviously just come out of the shower as his smooth thin chest still had droplets of water on it.

"What a gwaan, Saff," he greeted her in his accented English. "I wasn't expecting you back so early." He gathered her into his arms and hugged her tightly.

"I thought we could go out for dinner or something," she suggested. It felt weird being in his arms like this, but she hugged him back and readily accepted his light squeeze of affection.

"I'd better be going." The sharp-edged voice of the stranger cut in.

Roderick repositioned Saffron in his arms as they turned to face the other man.

"Jefferson, did you introduce yourself to my girl?" Roderick asked. Saffron warmed at being introduced as his girl.

"No," Jefferson said coldly.

"He let me in," Saffron acknowledged.

"Come meet her properly," Roderick said, drawing her closer. "Saffy, this is my friend Jefferson."

"Hello," Saffron said, walking forward with an extended hand.

Jefferson busied himself with his watch and turned away. Saffron wasn't quite sure if it was a deliberate snub as it was executed with smooth expertise.

"I'd better be going," Jefferson said, breaking the awkward silence. Completely ignoring Saffron, he turned towards Roderick to shake his hand.

Saffron turned away to go into her bedroom, failing to see the two men hug closely and the hostile look one of them sent her way.

∽∽∽

"Are you sure you don't want any more wine, Roderick?" Saffron asked, fracturing the silence. They were sitting on the couch. She'd changed and put on a pair of washed-out jeans that was once black but was now a soft grey, and a shell-pink spaghetti strapped top.

She'd teased him earlier, hoping he'd get the hint and put some clothes on. But he'd stubbornly refused, saying he was comfortable in the towel and that she'd actually seen him in less. Saffron had blushed. They may have once been lovers but that was a long time ago. Tomorrow, she realised, she'd have to set some ground rules, starting with clothes and then on to strangers in her home.

With her head in his lap, Roderick stroked Saffron's hair as they talked about the early days and life in Jamaica. It was an easy, undemanding atmosphere as they talked like old friends, drinking red wine and nibbling on slices of cold pizza they had ordered earlier.

Although the mood was nice and Saffron was content, she couldn't help but realise that Roderick hadn't kissed her properly since he'd arrived. Affectionate hugs and friendly kisses yes, but nothing deep and emotional. She desperately needed deep and emotional from him. She needed to feel the same kind of heat Lucas had made her feel last night. The time with Lucas was a moment of madness. She'd been lonely, he'd been lonely and they'd slept together. It didn't mean anything. The declaration of love was made in the heat of the moment. It couldn't mean anything, Saffron convinced herself as she snuggled into Roderick's side.

This was nice. No, it was more than that, it was almost like coming home, laying together, talking about nothing and everything. No pressure, she thought drowsily.

❧❦❧❦

A loud noise woke them, and together Roderick and Saffron sat up dazed as the room was flooded with bright fluorescent light.

"Let me guess?" Lucas mumbled, standing before them like a vengeful angel dressed in full black. "The fiancé has finally arrived!" he announced with theatrical flourish, sending Saffron a scathing look.

"Luc—" Saffron began, but he held up his hand, slashing it through the air as if cutting her to pieces.

"You can say nothing I want to hear," he said through gritted teeth. "You lied." Dropping his key to the carpet, he looked at her with raw pain before quickly trying to conceal it. "Enjoy your life," he said before slamming the door behind him.

With a gasp of distress, Saffron snatched up the key and moved blindly to the door.

"I tink you have some explaining to do, woman," Roderick said casually, holding Saffron's wrist and spinning her around to face him. For someone so slender he had a powerful grip, she thought, while trying to free herself from his grasp.

"What do you mean?" she asked. She didn't want to be here. She needed to go after Lucas.

"Mi tink someone been playing around," said Roderick.

"Lucas is a friend," Saffron said in defence, somewhat self-consciously.

"One, a friend who has his own key." Roderick held up his hand and checked off a finger. "Two, a friend who comes round when it's after midnight." He checked off another finger. "A friend who looked as though him ready to kill me." Another finger went down. "Saffy, you take man for an idiot."

"No, Roderick!" she exclaimed as she looked around for her shoes. "He's my best friend Lucas." Spying her trainers under the side table, she moved away to pull them out.

"No woman of mine going to have a man as a bloodclaat best friend! You forget who me is?"

"No." Pulling on her trainers, Saffron grabbed her bag and finally gave Roderick her attention. But she needed to go. She needed to get to Lucas. She couldn't deal with this kind of macho bull right now.

"He's my best friend," she repeated, not knowing why she should actually justify her relationship with Lucas to Roderick anyway.

"You can go back and sleep with him then. Me outs."

"Excuse me?" Saffron said puzzled, not understanding the phrase.

"Me gone. Me outs. Me don't want to crowd your space."

"You don't crowd my space."

"Woman, you know me better than most. Me don't come after no one."

She really didn't have time for this. Maybe she was a cold-hearted bitch, but she wanted to go to Lucas; he was her priority right now. She'd deal with Roderick later.

Roderick picked up an expensive mobile phone from the coffee table and punched in a number.

Saffron hadn't even noticed it as it was so slim and small. "Who are you ringing and where did you get that phone?" she asked suspiciously.

"Jefferson and Jefferson," Roderick replied with a shrug before going into Saffron's bedroom to take his flight bag out of her wardrobe, where he'd stashed it earlier.

"He gave it to you? Just who is he anyway? You never did say."

"You didn't ask."

Roderick swept the towel from his hips in a flamboyant manner and flashed a devilish grin before pulling on a pair of jeans.

"Who is he?" Saffron demanded again.

"A friend. He picked me up from the airport. We chilled out and then came up here."

Saffron looked at him with suspicion in her eyes.

"He picked you up? Why didn't you let me pick you up?"

"London too far, and me did want a day or so in the city for a time."

Saffron noticed that his Jamaican accent was getting stronger. She crossed her arms over her breasts. "Just how long have you been in England anyway?" she asked with sick unease.

Roderick pulled a thick jumper over his head, and Saffron couldn't help but notice that it was of a very high quality.

"A week or so," he answered.

"You've been here over a week and you're just coming up here?!" she fumed. "You didn't even ring me!"

Roderick finished dressing. "It's a good thing I was away. Maybe it would have been me seeing you sleeping with another man on your couch!"

Saffron stepped back as though she'd been slapped.

"How can you say that to me?"

"Easy. Gal, you too loose," he replied. "You make me come all dis way, and look, you fucking another rassclaat man!"

Saffron was taken back by his crudeness but flushed guiltily, knowing he was right.

Roderick gladly watched her hang her head in shame and pushed past her to walk out of the flat, slamming the door behind him.

Saffron laughed hysterically. She couldn't help herself. Two men in her life, and both had left slamming the door behind them. She laughed until the tears flowed. It had been an emotional day and she was rung out. She didn't know where Roderick had gone, and right now she didn't care. But at least Lucas was within reach. After splashing cold water on her tear-stained face she pulled on a baggy jumper and left her flat, slamming the door behind her as well.

୬ଏୢୢ

"Don't do this, Lucas," Saffron pleaded. "You're drunk. Maybe we should talk in the morning."

He laughed and, placing the bottle down with a gentle thud, stood to face her. "Why? Loverboy gone back to Jamaica already?" he teased.

"Yes. No," Saffron mumbled. "Shall I make you a coffee?" They were standing inside Lucas' coffee bar.

"You're a piece of work, you know that, don't you?" He didn't wait for her to answer. "A beautiful, heartless woman who plays men like they are fools," he added with a smile and stroked a long finger down her cheek.

"I don't," Saffron said defensively.

"You do," he countered. "Why did you come to my place last night, Saffron?" he asked abruptly, moving away and going to the small sink tucked behind the shiny wooden counter to pour himself a glass of water.

"I told you last night."

He switched on a light, bathing the counter in a soft yellow glow, which in turn cast shadows around the rest of the room.

"So what's up?" Lucas asked, turning to face her over the counter. "The fiancé wasn't up to scratch?" Saffron moved to hit him, but he caught her hand and shook his head.

"Tut, tut, you only get to hit me once, and you've already done that. But I could slap you bloody stupid!"

Saffron gasped. "I shouldn't have come," she uttered shakily, moving to the door. For the first time she was scared of the violence emanating from Lucas.

"No, you shouldn't!" he replied. "And don't you dare cower away as though I hit women!" He moved menacingly around the counter towards her.

"Lucas, I'm sorry I hurt you—"

"When did he come?" Lucas asked. Saffron shifted with guilty unease, unable to look at him. "My God! He was here last night, wasn't he?"

"No. Yes. He was here, but—"

"You screwed me and then you screwed him, and now you don't know who the hell you want! Jesus!" Lucas erupted, grabbing her shoulders and leading her backwards until she was trapped between the counter and his hard, heated body.

"You came for this, didn't you, Saffron?" Lucas breathed against her lips before lifting her onto the counter and wrapping her long legs around his waist. "This is what you want, isn't it, Saff?" he asked, touching her face lightly with his thumbs. "Go to your fiancé, Saffron." He nipped at her bottom lip, pulling on it gently. "But you will go with the memory of me inside you first!"

The kiss she expected, but the scorching heat that seared through her, she did not. His mouth was hard and sure, his kisses long and deep, intent on taking her over.

Saffron threw her head back and held onto his hair as he brought her even closer, massaging her bum through her jeans before skimming his hand across her front. She wanted desperately to feel his mouth there. She whimpered, lifting her hips, urging him on.

He laughed devilishly and pushed her backwards to gain access to her zip. Smoothing a hand on her stomach, he used his mouth to nuzzle open the snaps and push her jeans and lacy panties down.

She felt the cold night air across the top of her thighs as he stepped over her jeans and between her legs. He pulled her roughly to the edge of the counter.

Lucas held her gaze as he moved a finger against her swollen vagina, watching her gasp as her head fell back and she opened herself even further for him. He moved his finger back and forth, teasing the opening and loving when his finger glistened with her juice.

"Taste," he commanded, stroking his wet finger against her mouth. She shook her head. "Taste," he commanded again before smoothing his palm gently down her jumper, gliding beneath it to capture one of her nipples.

"You like that, don't you?" He didn't wait for an answer while continuing to tease her, rolling her nipple back and forth, watching her closely as she gasped with pleasure.

Lucas dropped his head to kiss her lady parts.

"Ah, Lucas," she moaned.

"That's right, honey. It's me, Lucas," he responded, breathing against her, loving the way her hips rocked against his mouth.

"Lucas."

He could feel the pressure building inside her and pushed a finger deep inside her moist and warm vagina, wanting to take her to the edge of ecstasy.

"Suck for me, Saffron," he ordered, tracing his wet finger against her lips. Saffron could smell the deep husky scent of herself on his finger and captured it between her teeth to suck it deeply into her mouth.

Their eyes locked, and she held his hand as she traced her tongue over his finger. His eyes darkened even more, and with her legs wrapped around him she urged him closer to kiss him deeply. But he pulled away, and laughing, scooped her up, turned her around and surged into her from behind.

Saffron gasped and was soon overcome by the hot pulsating friction that made her scream as she fell apart and he spilled into her with a strong and final thrust.

⁂

Lucas wrapped his arms around Saffron's waist and laid his head between her shoulder blades. They were both breathing heavily, and he could feel the rapid beat of her heart beneath his arms.

With grave reluctance he slipped out of her and pulled her close.

This was it, he thought grimly. He couldn't do it any more. Saffron took too much out of him. She didn't know what she wanted, and now that her boyfriend was here in Nottingham, where the hell did that leave him? No, this was it.

Saffron could feel him withdraw from her as she straightened. He gently turned her around and with great care and concentration pulled up her panties and then her jeans, fastening them before reaching up to cup her face with his hands.

Her lips were swollen, her hair a mess and her eyes bright. He took it all in, committing her lovely face to memory.

"Lucas?" Saffron muttered. The way he was looking at her was scaring her.

"Saff, it's your choice now, you—" Before he could finish, a commanding voice interrupted.

"Gianluca, pay the girl and get her out of here. I've given you long enough!"

Lucas and Saffron sprang apart. Whatever Lucas was about to say was forgotten as the bar was flooded with bright light. An old man leaning heavily on a cane stepped forward.

Saffron turned and looked at Lucas, surprised that he hadn't reprimanded the old man for insulting her. Instead, he stood frozen, as all the colour drained from his skin.

"Ah, so it was you I saw sniffing around the other day, Muzio? I see some things never change. Still his little lap dog," Lucas said, addressing the big dark-suited man who had entered behind the old man. "Go home, Saffron."

"What's going on? And who are they?" Saffron asked.

"Nothing to do with you," Lucas replied through gritted teeth.

"I don't understand."

"Get rid of your whore, Gianluca. We need to talk," the old man shouted impatiently.

"What do you want?" Lucas asked.

"I won't talk in front of the darkie," the old man replied.

Saffron gasped. He could not be referring to her! She glared at him and then back at Lucas, who did nothing! She'd had enough of this. Who was this man to call her names?

"How dare you!" she said finally, stepping forward, but Lucas's hand shot out and stilled her, swinging her around to face him.

"I need you to go home. Now," he said in a calm voice.

His voice was too calm and it frightened her. "I'm not leaving you," she replied.

Lucas watched her, and knowing the glint of defiance in the angle of her chin, forced himself to relax and smile. "It's all right," he soothed. "Go to my place and I'll be with you in a bit," he promised.

Saffron turned to go, and as she passed the old man she looked at him properly for the first time. He was almost as tall as Lucas, but his shoulders were bent with age. His hair was thick and silver. But it was the way he stared at her with his yellow eyes as though she was supposed to bow and scrape at his feet that she ultimately remembered.

"You're the man from the steps," she blurted.

"And you're the tramp who has been sleeping with my son!"

She gasped and looked at Lucas.

"I thought you said your father was dead?" she asked without thinking.

"He is to me," Lucas answered.

The old man cackled. "I see you're more like me than you want to be."

"I'm nothing like you!" Lucas shouted vehemently. "Nothing."

"Don't you raise your voice at me, boy," the old man warned, lifting his cane in a threatening manner. "I want to know why you went to a bank to borrow money! Embarrassing me like that!"

"Is this what the fatherly visit is about? Trying to save face, are you? What was it you used to say, family honour comes first?" Lucas retorted, laughing harshly. "You're a bloody joke. I don't want your money. I have my own."

"But obviously not enough that you have to go to another bank to borrow! When you own several yourself!"

Saffron gasped. What did the old man mean by Lucas owned a bank?

"That's right, girlie," the old man revealed with satisfaction. "You're bedding Gianluca Conti-Bridgewater, next in line to the Conti-Bridgewater Empire. Banks, hotels, electronics," he added with a shrug. "You name it and a Conti is behind it."

"I haven't been a Conti since the day I walked out of your house," said Lucas.

The old man laughed. "Who do you think owns this building? You're a Conti, and we Italians look after our own."

Lucas had gone white.

"It's time for you to get back to London. Playtime is over," the old man said.

"Forget it."

"You dare to tell me no?" the old man challenged, his face turning purple with rage.

"I want nothing to do with you or the family."

"Your mother will be hurt to hear you say that."

"You leave my mother out of this."

"You have commitments to others."

"I said no."

The old man nodded and Lucas watched him suspiciously. He had given up too easily, and the old man never gave in.

"Ok, you play with your little friend," he said, looking Saffron over as if contemplating a purchase. "Even I must admit she's a pretty one. Her breasts are a little small for my taste though." Swiftly the old man stretched a hand out and roughly fondled Saffron's breasts.

She pushed him away. At the same time Lucas came flying across the room and knocked the old man to the ground. Muzio suddenly pushed past Saffron and punched Lucas in the jaw, sending him crashing into the bar, before he swiftly went over to Lucas's father to gently lift him to his feet.

But Lucas's father had other ideas and shrugged him off.

"I see you still have it," he said, beaming gleefully. "This is who you are, boy! You have never felt more alive than you are right now." He reached into his jacket pocket and pulled out a white handkerchief to wipe the trickle of blood from the corner of his mouth.

"Already I have bought this building. I am buying your home. There will be nothing left for you in this city. Everywhere you go I will be with you. I have eyes everywhere. Every woman you want, I will bed. Even this one."

"Bed her. Girls like this are a penny each. Like you I like a little variety," Lucas declared, refusing to look at Saffron as he heard her stricken gasp.

The old man laughed. "See, you may not like me, but my blood flows in your veins. You are my son and you will come home."

"I'd rather see you dead than step foot in that house," Lucas exclaimed.

The old man laughed, flinging back his head.

"Such passion." He shook his head with regret. "You will do well to curb it in the boardroom, my son," he advised. "They'd eat you alive."

Lucas stiffened.

"I will tell your mother you send your love," the old man said.

He then left. Muzio gave Lucas a small nod before following behind his employer.

The room throbbed with deafening silence. Lucas moved to the door and locked it before retrieving his whisky and drinking it directly from the bottle. He stood in the middle of the room with the bottle raised to his lips and watched Saffron. This was what he'd never wanted her to know, and he could feel the millions of questions she wanted to ask. But he'd be dammed if he would answer any of them. She didn't deserve an explanation.

"Here," Lucas said, offering Saffron the bottle. "You look like you need it."

Saffron drank, gasped, and drank some more.

"Are you going to talk about it?" Saffron asked, noticing how his shoulders stiffened. He had retreated into that wall of his.

"No," he replied.

"I can't take it in."

"There is nothing for you to take in. This has nothing to do with you and who I am," he said harshly.

"Are you crazy?" she shouted at him. "You lied!"

"Only by omission."

"Telling me your father is dead is more than a general omission!"

"He is dead to me. Before tonight I'd not seen him in almost ten years."

"You worked three jobs to get through university when all this time you're a millionaire! Gianluca something or other. You even lied about your name!"

"What's in a name?" Lucas replied lightly. "And it's not my money, and working three jobs was nothing." He shrugged.

"I don't believe this." Saffron rubbed her tired, stinging eyes. "Are you going?"

"Going where?"

"Are you dense? To London."

"I hadn't planned to."

"But what about your mother?"

"I don't talk about her."

Saffron almost screamed in frustration. "Oh, for God's sake! If you don't want to talk about it just say so, and we'll go home."

Lucas stared at her for a long moment, the silence stretching and stretching like a bungee rope.

He looked at her quizzically. "Home, Saffron?" he asked eventually.

"Was I presuming too much, Lucas?"

"What do you think?"

"Look, will you stop answering a question with a question. It's driving me insane. I've had a rough day, okay. And I can't take any more." She was almost in tears. "I just can't," she whispered, gulping.

"I'll walk you home," Lucas offered.

"I want to go to yours."

Lucas knew Saffron was emotional and confused right now. But he needed her out of the way. His father played dirty and had blood on his hands; he would easily hurt her just to get at him.

"What we did tonight was goodbye."

A sharp pain buzzed through her. "You don't mean that," Saffron sobbed. "Not after what we just did."

"I do."

"But—"

"The fiancé is back, and I finally got what I waited a hell of a long time to get."

Saffron slapped him so hard that it marked his face. Lucas stood, staring at her. Only the vein throbbing on his forehead signalled his rage.

"I won't apologise," Saffron said.

"You never have, so why start now? I'll walk you home."

"Forget it. You know, I thought you were an honourable man."

Lucas laughed. "Don't use that word with me, Saffron, it will get you nowhere."

"Through the years I thought of you as many things," she said through her tears. "But to treat me like this. I mean more to you than this," she added, before gasping and grabbing his arm. "Is it because I'm black? Your father—"

"Don't be so bloody stupid!" Lucas shouted before she could finish.

"The problem is you're too damned spoilt. Everything you want you get. But not me."

"I won't beg," she promised, tears streaming down her face.

He stared down at her, his gold eyes boring into hers but giving nothing away.

"He was right, you know. You are like him. A cold, unfeeling bastard!" Saffron said. With that, she left.

&ニ&‿&ニ&

The urgent knocking on the front door roused Saffron from the couch.

"What!" she spat as she flung the door open. Her head ached and she wanted to sleep for days.

Cassidy held up her hands in defence.

"It's only me. Can I come in?" she asked her friend, who was blurry-eyed and leaning heavily against the door frame.

"Of course. Sorry," Saffron muttered.

Cassidy closed the door behind her and looked around. She had never seen Saffron's house in such a mess. Dirty clothes were piled high in one corner, empty tissue boxes laid on the table with crumpled used tissues around them, trailing onto the floor. Saffron was dressed in an old tracksuit that had seen better days. She flung herself onto the sofa and pulled a woolly blanket over her head. Cassidy sat down on a nearby low table, her forehead furrowed with concern.

"Are you poorly, Saff?" she asked.

"Mmm."

"Come on out from under there. I can't hear what you're saying," Cassidy ordered gently.

Saffron peeped from under the blanket, folded the edge under her chin and looked at Cassidy.

"Migraine."

"Have you taken something for it?" Cassidy asked.

"No."

"And why not? You know you have to catch it just as it starts," Cassidy said. "Would you like me to get some tablets for you?"

"No. I'll be ok."

Looking at Cassidy properly for the first time, Saffron noticed the plaster on her arm. "What the hell happened to you?" she asked sternly.

Cassidy frowned, looking at the plaster that extended from her knuckles all the way up past her elbow. "I had an accident at work."

"At the bakery?"

"No, they fired me, remember," Cassidy reminded her friend. "No, the factory."

"How?"

"Doesn't matter really. They were really nice about it and called the ambulance. One of the machines malfunctioned and instead of grabbing the cardboard box like it's supposed to, it grabbed my sleeve and twisted my arm around."

Saffron gasped. "God, that must have hurt."

"Before I knew what happened, my arm was dangling around my ankles," Cassidy joked.

"It's not funny. What did the factory say?"

"They were great. I can have as much time off as I want and still get paid."

"The factory is being so nice so you'll feel guilty and not take them to court," Saffron told her friend.

"I'm not taking them to court."

"Yes, you are! They were responsible for you and the machinery you work on. You will be compensated for this." Saffron flung the blanket aside and stood up to stretch. This was just what she needed; a distraction.

"Oh," Cassidy replied.

"Oh, indeed." Saffron flashed her friend a smile. "I've got this friend who's big in the compensation claim thingy arena. I'll give her a ring and arrange a meeting."

Saffron left Cassidy to go into her bedroom. Cassidy tidied up the place a bit, which was a bit awkward to do with one hand, especially since she was left-handed, and it was her left arm that was in the cast.

"Ok, that's all set. We have an appointment next week at ten, down in London," said Saffron upon returning to the room.

"Aren't you going into the shop?" Cassidy asked.

"Mairead is there. She's been looking after the place these last few days."

Cassidy frowned. Saffron was a dot short of a control freak. Letting Mairead look after the shop was unusual, though Mairead was quite capable. Cassidy looked at Saffron properly. Noticing the dark circles under her eyes, which looked swollen and red as if she'd been crying. Her hair was in its usual ponytail, but it had no healthy lustre.

"Ok. What's up?" asked Cassidy.

"Nothing."

Cassidy raised a narrow blonde eyebrow and waited.

Saffron, noticing that look, gave in and told Cassidy everything.

"...And now, looking at the papers, he's in London."

"And all this happened when?" Cassidy asked, stunned. She'd actually gone down to Lucas's place for a coffee last night, but it was closed. A sign on the door stated that it was shut for refurbishment until further notice.

"A week ago. And look at this." Saffron dug deep into the side of the sofa and pulled out a twisted newspaper.

Lucas's picture was on one side and his father on the other. The headline paid tribute to his father, who had died in a car crash on the M1 after paying his son a visit. Gianluca, as the paper called Lucas, had now suddenly reappeared and was running his father's conglomerate.

"Lucas?" Cassidy asked, shocked. "Our Lucas?"

Saffron nodded. "He's not taking any of my calls."

"Our Lucas is this Gianluca?" Cassidy asked again. "Unbelievable."

"Isn't it? He's lied to us all this time, Cass. I feel so betrayed."

Cassidy didn't know what to say. She felt the same. But then, she wasn't in love with him.

"There's more, Cass," Saffron said. She told her about them becoming lovers and Roderick being here in England.

"What, he's here now?" Cassidy looked around as though expecting Roderick to appear out of the woodwork.

"I don't know what to do."

"Well, naturally, you have to see and speak to Lucas—"

"But he's not taking my calls," Saffron said.

"Go down to London for a few days," Cassidy encouraged. "After all these years together you can't leave it like this. You love him, don't you?"

"As a friend."

Cassidy laughed. "Who are you trying to fool? You've always loved him but held on to Roderick as an escape route to your feelings."

"That's not true!" shouted Saffron.

"Course it is. I don't see you crying over Roderick. Are you?"

That remark was greeted by silence.

"I have feelings for Roderick," Saffron admitted reluctantly.

Cassidy sighed. She wasn't very good with this love thing herself. The one time she fell in love, she got pregnant. The father went missing, only showing up when the baby was several months old to kidnap him. She'd never seen either of them again.

"I don't know what to say," said Cassidy.

"How about we sort out your compensation thing first, and take it from there. Who needs men?" Saffron declared, throwing the newspaper into the waste paper basket. "Let's go out for dinner. I'm starved."

Cassidy picked up the paper, reread it properly and made a note of the company Lucas now headed.

She would do this one thing for Saffron.

⁂

"Someone to see you, sir," the disembodied voice said from the little box on his desk. Lucas wanted to smash the damn thing.

"I said I do not want to be disturbed."

Lucas heard a scuffle and then the door to his office burst open.

"Cassidy?" he asked in amazement, rising from behind the huge, menacing desk that used to be his father's.

"I'm sorry, sir, she just..." the secretary tried to explain.

"It's okay, Mrs. Tunnock," Lucas said, dismissing the other woman as he walked over to Cassidy. She looked out of place in the dark intimidating office, which boasted heavy mahogany furniture and panels on the wall.

Lucas smiled. He wanted to give Cassidy a hug, but he knew she didn't go in for that kind of thing.

"It's good to see you, Cassidy," he said.

She was dressed in blue jeans and a blue anorak. Her hair was pulled back in its usual style, accentuating her eyes and her pale, thin face.

"It's good to see you, too."

Lucas cleared his throat. "Would you like to sit down?" he offered, gesturing to the dark leather chair. The deep chair swamped Cassidy's small frame. "How can I help you?" asked Lucas.

Cassidy looked down at her hands, unsure of where to start. She noticed that her knuckles were red from the cold. She really would have to buy herself a pair of gloves, she thought.

"I was in London and thought I'd pop round."

Lucas looked at her. Cassidy barely left the East Midlands, much less to make it down to the capital for anything. But he thought he'd indulge her. He relaxed into his father's chair, for once not feeling the menacing weight of his responsibilities.

"Oh yeah?"

"I'm meeting this new private investigator," replied Cassidy.

"Private investigator?"

"You know, for looking for my son."

"What son?"

"Billal."

Lucas sat forward with alertness. "I think you'd better start from the beginning."

Cassidy did. From the very beginning. She hadn't realised that all this time Lucas didn't know about the kidnapping. Saffron had been true to her word and hadn't told a soul.

They were interrupted a few times by Lucas' secretary reminding him of the meeting he had scheduled. But for the most part, she had his undivided attention.

"And that's about it," Cassidy said, almost an hour later.

"My God. I knew something was up, but never that. You should have told me."

Cassidy flushed. "I'm so used to relying on myself," she said, shrugging her narrow shoulders. "It was nothing personal."

Lucas smiled. "No offence taken. Now, Cass, before you say no, would you do me the honour and have dinner with me?"

"Sorry. I'm heading back up to Nottingham on the train tonight."

"You can stay at my place," he persuaded. "It's this huge, ugly monstrosity that I rattle around in on my own."

"I couldn't," she replied, biting her lip with indecision.

"Course you can. It would help me get my mind off all of this." Lucas swept up an arm, indicating the desk strewn with papers, a computer and the rest of the room. "Please."

Cassidy smiled. "Will you make me a cappuccino?"

Lucas laughed the kind of laugh she was used to hearing from him. "Of course. Let's go," he replied.

❧⨾❧⨾❧

The house was indeed an ugly monstrosity. But Cassidy was too polite to say so. Lucas had a gleam in his eyes as though he knew what she was thinking.

The house was built of old, dark stones and the wings on each side had obviously been added within the past several years. The design was out of sync with the rest of the building. Huge stone gargoyles peered down from the slate roof. Cassidy felt like she was entering Hell and couldn't believe Lucas had been brought up in this dark and dismal place.

"Come on," Lucas prompted, opening the heavy wooden door with a gilded key.

The hallway was huge, dominated by a heavy chandelier with hundreds and hundreds of crystals dangling from it.

"I'm glad I don't have to clean that," Cassidy exclaimed. Lucas burst out laughing.

"Cass, it is so good to have you here. It really is," he reiterated, flinging a door open and ushering her inside.

The room was long and narrow, with an open fireplace at one end, which was lit. Cassidy turned to look at Lucas.

"There's a butler, cook and other staff somewhere about the place," he explained.

"You really grew up here?" Cassidy asked, looking around the imposing room with amazement.

He nodded. "I hated it. I left as soon as I could." He walked over to the window and looked out at the extensive gardens, where every blade of grass was the exact length as its neighbour, and the rose bushes stood in a straight line.

"Okay, we've talked about everything and everyone except Saffron," Cassidy said later as their plates were being cleared away by a maid in uniform.

Lucas's eyes narrowed and looked at her quizzically. "You know?" he asked.

"She told me everything," said Cassidy.

"Everything?"

Cassidy nodded.

"Then I guess you know the fiancé is here."

"In England yes, but nearer to you than to Saffron."

"I don't understand," said Lucas.

"He's in London."

"Since when?"

"Ask Saffron."

"I'm asking you."

"He never stayed the night there," Cassidy replied.

Lucas felt a surge of relief and then remembered seeing them together on the couch. Roderick had nothing on, and Saffron had had her head buried in his groin. That told it's own story.

"Tell me about this private investigator of yours, Cass," Lucas said, changing the subject abruptly. "He doesn't sound very reputable."

With a searching look, Cassidy answered, knowing the subject of Saffron and Roderick was now out of bounds.

❧❦❦❧

"I'm going to India," Cassidy announced to Saffron a week later. They were having lunch at a small restaurant upstairs the Victoria Centre shopping mall.

"Excuse me?" Saffron said, not sure she'd heard right.

"India. Gianluca hired a new private investigator, and he's already got a strong lead after only a week!" Cassidy gushed excitedly to her friend.

"Gianluca?"

"You know exactly who I'm talking about. Lucas!"

"When did you see him?" Saffron enquired, chasing a king prawn around her plate.

"When I went to London to see that solicitor. I stopped by," Cassidy revealed. Saffron had been ill.

Saffron stabbed the prawn and bit into it, only to grab a napkin and spit it out. It tasted foul.

"Oh. That's nice," she said.

"Don't you want to know what about?"

"Not particularly, no," Saffron said sharply, immediately regretting her harshness. Cassidy deserved more from her. But where was her loyalty? Saffron had stood by her side and helped her all these years and all of a sudden, Lucas, no Gianluca, as he now calls himself, was flavour of the month!

"I'm sorry," Saffron apologised, seeing the hurt on her friend's face. She cited the continuous migraine as her excuse.

Cassidy accepted the explanation and excitedly went on with her story, but Saffron only gave her half an ear. Lucas had hired a new investigator and a lead had come up, and Cassidy would be leaving for India in three days.

Aware of the long silence that followed, Saffron looked up to see Cassidy staring at her expectantly.

"Sorry, I missed that."

"You can come to India with me," Cassidy invited eagerly.

"India?"

"Yeah. It would be good to have someone with me."

"I can't, Cass," replied Saffron.

"You really need to get out of this slump you've let yourself slip into," Cassidy warned.

"I'm not in a slump."

"Course you are. You've lost weight, you haven't any make-up on and you're not happy for me."

Guiltily, Saffron reached across the table and took her friend's hand.

"I am, Cass, really I am," she beseeched passionately. "But I just don't want you to get your hopes up again, that's all." She squeezed Cassidy's hand, willing her to understand. "I think you should stop looking for him and start living again. Smarten yourself up and find yourself a boyfriend and perhaps have another child."

All the blood drained from Cassidy's already pale face as she looked at her friend in shock.

"You want me to give up?" Cassidy whispered in disbelief. "You think I shouldn't go but wonder for the rest of my life if it was him?"

"You've been on your own for so long," Saffron argued. "You followed a little boy into his house, for goodness sake. That's not what rational people do!"

Cassidy stood up to go. She was disappointed.

"Thanks a lot, Saff. You're supposed to be happy for me. I'm finally making headway." She shook her head and threw down a ten pound note on the table. "That's for my half of lunch."

Cassidy pulled on her anorak with sharp angry movements, her face flushed with pain and her eyes filled with tears. "You've changed and it's not for the better!" Cassidy said, then left the restaurant to merge with the afternoon lunch crowd.

Brilliant, Saffron thought to herself. Just brilliant. She really was the selfish bitch Lucas had said she was.

*S*affron Noble never thought her life would have changed so much. Ten months ago she was engaged and living in Nottingham with a nice flat and an established business. She had even been nominated for the East Midlands Business Woman of The Year award. She had a great social life and a circle of friends she cherished. But everything had changed within a matter of hours.

The fist patter of rain hit the dusty ground at her sandaled feet and was quickly followed by another and another. Saffron moved onto the verandah and sat on the top step to watch the downpour.

It never seized to amaze her how hard and fast the rain falls in Jamaica. Roads were regularly washed away during showers. And whenever she visited her relatives up in Long Road, Portland, she was amazed at how much of the land had been eroded by the rain. Houses had been lost. Huge gorges resulted where rainwater cut lethal paths down the mountainside. Most of the young people had left to find work in the tourist areas or Kingston, the capital city. There was no one young enough left to farm the land.

Saffron let out a sigh. Lucas. He was never far from her thoughts. The last time they were together had been explosive. Both of them said horrible things to each other.

She had eventually gone down to London months later. She'd felt increasingly guilty about the way she had treated Cassidy and wanted to get in touch with her, but the only way to do that was to go and see Lucas.

She'd just showed up at his office as previous attempts to make an appointment had been repeatedly blocked by his secretary. He'd apparently blacklisted her name. But she'd made it up to the executive floor, only to be stopped just as she was about to barge into his office.

The secretary, a tall curvaceous redhead, had ordered her to sit on one of the chairs in the reception area while she phoned him.

So Saffron sat and patiently waited, dressed in a grey suit, silky cream camisole, high heels and full make-up.

She waited for three and a half hours. Hungry and growing angry, she got up and marched into his office and slammed the door shut. She expected to find him surrounded by executives as she was led to believe. Instead, he was staring into space with his feet on the desk crossed at the ankles.

"What happened to the meeting you were supposed to be having?" she inquired.

Lucas looked at her, his golden eyes pinning her in place. There were lines of strain around his eyes, she noticed, and the groves beside his mouth had deepened. He looked at least five years older than his actual age.

"What are you doing here?" he asked, going over to the drinks cabinet and pouring himself a glass of an amber liquid from a square crystal decanter.

"You wouldn't take my phone calls, so I had no choice."

He raised an eyebrow and slowly looked her over before sitting on the corner of his desk to face her. His hard thigh was so close she could see the outline of muscle and had to sit on her hands to keep from touching him.

"I need to find Cassidy," Saffron said.

"And here I am thinking you came for yourself," he taunted casually. "But then, we all have first-hand experience of just how self-absorbed you can be."

"That's not a fair thing to say."

"Oh yeah? Cassidy was here in floods of tears, not wanting to go to India because you said she might get hurt. And you think that's not selfish?"

"It's not what I meant!"

"You'd rather she spend the rest of her life looking for her son, working three, four jobs to pay countless investigators who have been ripping her off for years!"

Saffron felt overcome with guilt. "She'd caught me at a bad time..."

Lucas made a slashing movement with his arm.

"Don't you do that at me!" Saffron yelled, thoroughly incensed. "I'd just found out my best friend had lied to me all these years, my engagement was all but over and Cassidy had decided to swan off to India, when for the first time ever I needed her!"

Lucas drained his glass and moved to the bar again. The silence was interrupted by the ping ping of crystal touching crystal.

"When did you start drinking so much?" she asked, calming down. Her question was greeted by a casual shrug.

"Oh, I don't know," he replied, giving her a lopsided smile. "Since maybe I killed my father."

Saffron gasped. "Don't be ridiculous. You weren't even in the car."

"Ah, but you were there, weren't you, Saffron. With your panties still wet from our sex. You heard the last thing I said."

Saffron frowned, trying to remember.

Lucas sat down across from her with the wide, highly polished expanse of the dark desk between them. He stared at her, as if he was trying to see inside her head.

"I told him I'd rather he be dead."

"That's just talk. You didn't mean it."

"Ah, but I did," he laughed. "Now look at me." He gestured to his black suit, white shirt and muted tie. "The bastard probably crashed on purpose because here I am exactly where he wanted me to be. Trapped in his world and responsible for thousands and thousands of people who hated him!"

Saffron could see the pain Lucas was trying desperately to hide. "I'm sorry, Lucas."

He laughed. "And what have you got to be sorry for?"

"For all of this." Saffron waved her arm around the room.

Lucas rubbed his eyes tiredly. "Why are you really here? And don't give me the bull about Cassidy. I know you too well."

Saffron licked her lips and did it again when his gaze lowered. He still wanted her.

She uncrossed her long legs and walked around to sit on the corner of his side of the desk.

"I came to apologise for all the things I said that night."

"So you tracked me down. Well, Saff, apology accepted. Now, if you don't mind," Lucas said, checking his watch with a quick flick of the wrist. "I've got a plane to catch."

"That's it!" she shouted, standing over him. Lucas rocked back in the deep leather chair and looked at her totally unmoved by her tantrum.

"Calm down," he instructed.

"I won't calm down!" Saffron stomped a foot so hard the heel on her shoe broke. She kicked it off impatiently. "I came down here because I needed to talk to you, to see how you were doing after all these weeks. We used to be friends."

Then she stopped and looked at him, her eyes widening in shock, as she came to a sudden realisation.

"It was all a joke to you, wasn't it?" she whispered.

"Don't be ridiculous. And stop wasting my time," Lucas said and stood up to loom over her.

"Your life in Nottingham, it was all a big lie. You lied to us all, to me, to Cass, everyone. What did you do when you went home at night? Think about how you could dupe us, unsophisticated country folk again?"

"Stop being so bloody ridic–"

"Don't you dare say ridiculous again!" Saffron shouted, trying to hold the tears back. "I was your friend and you used me to get back at your father. We dreamed together, Lucas, worked hard together. I was with you when you bought your first suit, and all the while you were lying to me."

She was crying and she didn't care.

"I lied to protect you," Lucas shot back.

"Boy, oh boy, that is some excuse you've got going there, Lucas. It's so good I could even clap." And she did. A loud empty clap that bounced around the room.

"Stop it."

"It's so bloody brilliant. And you have the audacity to call me a liar, when you're the biggest one of all!"

She picked up her cream leather bag from the floor and turned to flounce out of his office when he suddenly dragged her to him and kissed her.

They had sex on the office desk. No preliminaries, no caresses. Just the hungry coupling of two people who were no longer friends.

"I don't ever want to see you again," Saffron said from the doorway minutes later. Black tracks of mascara stained her cheeks, a button was missing from her jacket, and she only had on one shoe.

"Be careful what you wish for, Saffron," Lucas replied with eyes dark with pain. "I know better than most that it can come true."

That was the last time Saffron had seen Lucas. She'd sold the shop to Mairead and leased the flat. Within two weeks, she was in Jamaica. And here she was five months later, still playing tourist and visiting sights as if she had all the time in the world.

The rain was finally slowing. Wafts of steam rose from the ground. Saffron smiled. Jamaica. How she loved this country. Nothing could compare to the vibrancy of the island. Everything was sharp, bright and poetic.

She wished Cassidy was here. Again she felt a pang of guilt for the way she had treated her friend. Looking back, she could see how her words must have hurt, and she sincerely regretted them. At the time she'd been jealous. Something was finally going right for Cassidy while her life was falling apart. It had never been like that. She was everything Lucas said she was, Saffron thought. Selfish and self-absorbed. What she needed to do was to go back to basics, and here, the country that helped shape her, was the right place to do so.

෨෬ஂ෬

Saffron stood on the verandah, after a long day and took in the scenery. Large ferns, flame red heliconias and vibrant wild orchids grew in abundance on the circumference of her property, shielding it from the road.

From the day she'd signed on the dotted line, the neighbourly Mas Arthur had appointed himself foreman, and the refurbishment had been done in record time. Two months later, she was able to move in.

Mas Arthur was her closest neighbour who lived on the incline a little way above her, here in Portland. It was comforting to know he could look down on her house.

She went inside, passing the original stone fireplace they were able to save to go to the small kitchen in the back to get the glass of lemonade she had made earlier. She set it down on the white wrought-iron table and went to wait for Mas Arthur on the verandah.

He rounded the corner, a sack slung over his shoulder. Saffron tried to tell him to slow down, that for a man his age he should be taking it easy. Offended, he puffed up his chest and told her that he was as young as he felt and that was not a day over forty.

Placing the sack on the bottom steps, he tipped his hat to her politely before using a blue rag to wipe the sweat from his face. He brushed off his trousers with his hands to get rid of some of the grass and mud clinging to them before sitting down.

"We never did get that rain, Mas Arthur," Saffron said.

"Don't worry, it will come. Portland hardly see a day without some," he stated expertly. "I brought up some corn from down the field."

"Thanks. I'll cook them with dinner," replied Saffron.

"No rush, but you need to go down to the church hall now. Them in the shop tell me to tell you that some foreigner going to build a hotel down pon di beach."

"Which beach?"

"Di local beach, Missy."

"I didn't know it was for sale again, and didn't the church say it wouldn't sell?" Saffron asked.

"So me did think too. Maybe dem get an offer too good fi let pass."

"So we have another hotel chain wanting to buy up our land. And where are we supposed to go and fish and swim?"

"Dat's why them at the shop want you to go to the meeting. I will stay here until Miss Hyacinth come."

"Thanks, Mas Arthur," said Saffron.

The locals had unofficially nominated Saffron as the town spokesperson. The mayor actually lived in Moore Town, deeper in the parish, and was of little use to them here on the coast.

"I'd better go and get ready." She went inside and surveyed her closet. Gone were the expensive jeans, dresses, jewellery and perfume. Saffron had simplified her life and her wardrobe. Shorts of varying lengths, skinny vests, simple sandals and flip flops were all she wore.

Saffron pulled on a pair of knee-length shorts and a plain top, shoved her feet into a pair of locally made leather flip flops and went to wash her face.

She no longer wore make-up and kept her hair in long natural twists that reached her shoulders.

She could hear Mas Arthur talking, and she quickly sprayed mosquito repellant all over herself, checked the other bedroom and stepped out of the house. After leaving a few instructions with Miss Hyacinth, Saffron set off with a determined march down the lane.

∞∞∞∞

Gianluca Conti-Bridgewater watched as Dean, his solicitor, nervously came forward. "We have a problem, sir."

"Deal with it," Gianluca replied. He was feeling unusually restless and would have preferred to be in bed with long-legged Rebecca, his latest girlfriend, although he was beginning to get a little tired of her. He checked his watch for the date. She'd been in his bed two months. It was time for him to send the roses and a bracelet from Tiffany's as a parting gift before she got too cosy.

Looking up from his computer, he realised Dean was still standing by the door as if ready to bolt. Gianluca flung down his gold pen and watched him, his brow furrowed with annoyance. Dean reluctantly came forward with a yellow folder held closely to his chest.

"What is it?" Gianluca asked impatiently. He didn't like being bothered by petty things.

Dean swallowed. "We went to Jamaica, sir, to buy the property you wanted. But we have strong opposition from the locals."

"Build them a school or something. I want that land," Gianluca ordered, turning back to his paperwork.

"They don't want someone from the outside building on it, sir."

"How much do I pay you?" Gianluca breathed in and then out very slowly before looking at the younger man with darkened eyes. Dean shifted nervously and answered him.

"And don't you think that with that kind of wage you should be able to sort it out?" Gianluca asked casually.

"Sir, I'm afraid it's not as simple as that," Dean went on.

He could feel a trickle of sweat run down his spine. "Sir, we-well, I spoke to the last person who was trying to p-purchase it, an American, and he said they set the obeah man on him, sir." Beads of sweat now dotted Dean's upper lip. He didn't brush them away.

"Excuse me?"

"Obeah, sir," Dean stuttered.

"Explain."

"Witchcraft, sir," Dean rushed on. "The American said he slept on his yacht that night and could hear things, sir!"

Gianluca made a sound that could almost be construed as a laugh.

"Jamaica is not Haiti, Dean. They don't practise witchcraft."

"But, sir, if you excuse me for saying so I spoke to a—" Dean fumbled with the folder he held and looked in it. "A Miss Noble, their spokesper—"

Gianluca sat up, giving Dean his full attention.

"Is something the matter, sir?"

"What did this woman look like?"

"I have some pictures, sir," Dean mumbled. "And some information on her here, sir." He stepped forward and slid the folder across his boss desk with relief.

Gianluca was reluctant to open it. He hadn't thought about her in years, and just hearing the name brought back a time he wanted to forget. But she wouldn't be living in rural Jamaica. He'd picked that location for its seclusion. It was well off the tourist map. And she must be married, living in Nottingham with five kids by now. She always said she wanted a large family.

"Leave me," he said sternly, dismissing Dean, who looked at him strangely before practically falling over his feet in haste to get out of the office.

Gianluca fingered the folder and held it between his thumb and forefinger. He then slammed it down to look out the window. It was snowing again. The large, thick flakes settled on the streets of New

York. He hated New York. The only place he really liked these days was his mother's little cottage in Italy.

He smiled at the thought of his beautiful mother finally enjoying her life and painting. His father had tried but never managed to break her spirit.

Turning to look at the folder, he chided himself for being so ridiculous. So what if it was Saffron? She was nothing to him.

Later, he opened the file and stopped breathing.

Within the hour he was airborne, on his way to Jamaica, in a murderous mood.

Chapter Five

S affron was busily hanging sheets on the long clothes line tied between an ackee tree and a tall breadfruit tree at the back of the house. It was another beautiful day, and she appreciated the swiftness with which her laundry dried crisply under the warm sun.

She was running low on tin food and other essentials and that meant a trip into Ocho Rios. She reached into the wicker basket at her feet to take out a white sheet, shaking it out before slinging it over the line and securing it with several wooden clothes pegs.

"Ahhh!" she screamed when she looked up and saw a man looking at her. "Roderick," she said in amazement. "My God, you frightened me!"

"Hiya, Saffy."

Moving around the sheet, she walked towards him.

"What are you doing here? And how did you find me?" He looked exactly the same, although not as lanky.

"I didn't know you were lost," Roderick replied.

"You know what I mean."

"Whew, it's hot, can we go inside? The heat is killing me," he said, pinching his off-white linen shirt between finger and thumb and pulling it away from his chest.

Saffron sighed dramatically. This was the fist time she was seeing Roderick since that night almost two years ago. She hadn't forgotten the awful things he had said.

"Oh, all right," she relented, leading the way to the kitchen. She didn't want to prolong his visit. She stood with her back to the sink and folded her arms across her chest.

Roderick raised his eyebrows enquiringly at her lack of hospitality.

"Should I take it that I'm not a welcomed guest?" he asked in a British accent that caused Saffron to look over Roderick's shoulder to see if Prince Philip had spoken instead.

"Let's just say I'd rather finish hanging out my washing," she answered.

Roderick chuckled, fished into the pockets of his linen trousers and pulled out a white handkerchief. "I come in peace," he said with a theatrical wave and a cheeky grin.

"Oh, all right." Saffron moved to the tiny fridge and opened it. "I can offer you water or home-made lemonade."

"Water, please."

She took out one of the many plastic jugs of boiled, partly frozen water and poured a generous amount into a tall plastic cup.

She caught Roderick looking at the cup ruefully, but he said nothing. He drank the water thirstily then held out the cup for more.

"Splendid. I needed that. I had certainly forgotten how incredibly hot the Caribbean can be."

Saffron laughed and walked him through the house, out onto the verandah, where they sat down.

"So," she began after a few minutes of uncomfortable silence, "what have you been doing with yourself? Obviously you live in England."

"Yes, it's my first time back since I left," Roderick answered.

Saffron smiled but said nothing.

"I'm doing law at Kingston University and working part-time at Jefferson's firm."

Saffron was surprised. She certainly wasn't expecting him to be at university.

"That's great," she said, not quite hiding the amazement in her voice.

He looked at her sideways, and then suddenly reached out to hold her rough work hands.

"I came to say sorry," he said.

"For what?"

"Taking advantage of you the way I did. Saffron, you've been a good friend. But friends were all we were going to be. I didn't feel the spark, and if you admit it, neither did you."

"I guess you knew that way before I did, Roderick." She moved her hands from his. "Why did you let me believe I meant more to you for all those years?"

"I do care. But not like that." Roderick stood up and looked out at the view. "I was feeling pressured by my mother to get married, and it certainly seemed easier to just go on with the charade for a while. But before I knew it, years had gone by, and then you issued that ultimatum."

He shrugged and turned to her, giving her a beseeching look. "I'm terribly sorry. I'm not proud of how I treated you, and I promise to give back every pound you gave me."

Saffron didn't know what to say. It seemed like such a long time ago, and it didn't factor into who she was now. It didn't matter. He didn't matter. She had never been happier since her move back to Jamaica and she told him so.

Roderick's shoulders sagged with relief, and it was only then she realised how guilty he must have been feeling. She knew how the heavy weight of guilt felt as she had carried it around with her everyday, knowing just how badly she had treated Cassidy.

"I know you left Nottingham not long after I came. So I thought..." Roderick hung his head in shame. Saffron joined him at the railing.

"No, my move here had nothing to do with us, but there—" A sudden movement in the bushes near the bottom of the hill caught her eye, but remembering that Mas Arthur sometimes tied the goats there, she dismissed it. "Remember Lucas?" she continued.

"The guy who came into your flat the same night I got there? The one you said was your best friend?"

Saffron nodded, taking his hand. "I'll show you."

With his soft hand within hers, she walked him into the house and into the bedroom.

There, sleeping peacefully with fingers in their mouths, were her children.

"This is my daughter Bella," she said with a proud whisper. "And this is Nico, my son. My twins."

Seeing that Roderick was about to start talking, she quickly ushered him out of the room and quietly pulled the door up behind them.

The twins would be a nightmare later if they didn't get enough nap time.

"You were pregnant when I was there?" Roderick asked with a disapproving, bullish look.

"Don't be stupid," she chided. "You had already left by the time they were conceived."

"But, my God, Saffy. How on earth have you been managing?"

"I bought this place," she said, looking around with pride. "And I get the rent money for the flat in England every month.

"But two kids, Saff? It can't be easy."

"I get help and, at the moment, I'm managing just fine."

"Do you need money, Saff? I mean as nice as this place is, it's a far cry from what you're used to," Roderick said cautiously.

Saffron smiled and sighed deeply. "Roderick, it's about going back to basics. I don't need all the trendy clothes and flashy jewellery any more. I'm happy with what I've got. Two healthy children and the support of the community." She smiled brightly, but Roderick was not convinced.

"But what about the father? The so-called best friend?" he asked.

Saffron shrugged and a faraway look came into her eyes.

"Is it okay if I stay the night?" Roderick asked, realising Saffron needed someone to talk to. "I'll sleep on the sofa or something?" he added quickly, seeing her shocked expression.

"Of course. I've got a spare room you could use, but I need to go into Ocho Rios to get some groceries."

"I'll do that." Roderick kissed her on the cheek before going down the shallow steps to his rental, which was parked beside her small car. "I'll bring dinner back," he said with a wave before driving off.

❧ ❦ ❧ ❦

Dinner was jerk chicken and pork with a huge loaf of freshly baked hardough bread, with grapenut ice-cream for dessert. Roderick offered to bathe the children while Saffron took a break.

Hearing all the giggles, she wondered who was having more fun. When bath time was over, Saffron dried and powdered the children before putting them to bed and covered the cot with a mosquito net.

She was reading by kerosene lamp the English newspaper Roderick had brought, when a sweeping light coming up the hill drew her attention. On occasion she'd had to redirect a lost tourist, so thinking nothing of it, she put the paper down and went out to the verandah.

The night air smelt heavily of jasmine, and Saffron drew in a long, deep and appreciative breath. It was pitch black outside as she didn't have any street lights and there was no moon. But Saffron took delight in seeing the tiny green flashing lights of the peenie wallies as they danced to their own rhythm around the bushes.

A large, dark four-wheel drive drew up beside the house. The driver switched off the engine. She couldn't see who was inside as the windows were heavily tinted. For a moment she felt a little apprehensive, but then she remembered that Roderick was inside the house, and Mas Arthur was within calling distance.

The rear door opened, and Saffron was able to make out a tall, shadowy figure.

"I think you may have lost your way," she called out in a friendly tone. "You came off the main road. This is a private house."

The figure didn't move and she realized that the person was able to see her clearly by the orange glow of light shining from the living room.

Lucas walked towards her, seeing the alarm on her face as he came nearer. He was so angry he could break her neck. He walked into the pool of light at the bottom of the steps and stopped. He watched with pleasure as the blood drained from Saffron's face. She swayed in shock, grabbing onto the wooden railing for support.

"Lucas?"

"At least you still remember my name," he responded, climbing the steps. Saffron moved backwards, blocking the doorway with a hand on each frame.

"Am I not welcome, Saffron?"

"No, yes...please," she mumbled. "What are you doing here?"

He looked at her naked feet and then took his own sweet time, looking at her long legs, past the faded shorts up to the simple white vest she wore. She knew she looked dirty. She hadn't showered all day.

"You look different," Lucas observed.

"Yes well—" Saffron couldn't get past the thought that Lucas was actually here and that Roderick was inside the house.

"Aren't you going to invite me in, Saffron? Or have you forgotten all aspects of polite civilization as well?"

Saffron gasped. If Lucas had remained in the shadows and spoken she would have assumed it was his father who was there talking to her like that. She folded her arms defensively.

"It's late," she said.

"It's barely eight o'clock."

"We go to bed early in the country."

Lucas stepped even closer, and she was able to see the changes in him. His hair was cut in a I-am-a-busy-tycoon style. She hated it. He looked thinner, with deep lines around his eyes and mouth. His mouth was set in a tight line, as though he had forgotten how to smile or he was now too busy to do so.

"Why don't you come back in the morning?" Saffron suggested nervously. "Then we can talk."

Lucas frowned. "Is there something or someone you're hiding in there, Saffron?" he asked with narrowed eyes. Deep inside, he wanted her to be honest and tell him about the child.

She took a moment to look at him. "No, it's just that—"

"Hey, Saffy, don't you have any hot water?" Roderick called out.

Saffron blushed, and then realizing she had nothing to feel guilty about, she told Lucas to stay on the verandah.

He followed her inside. Roderick was standing in the middle of the living room, wet and practically naked, with a small towel wrapped around his middle area. It was the same scene but different location from the last time the three of them had been in the same room together.

"So this is what you didn't want me to see!" Lucas bellowed, grabbing her wrist and swinging her around to face him.

"Get your hand off me! You've got no right to barge in here and accuse me of anything."

"I have every right!"

"I'd get out of here, old chap, if you want to live," Roderick warned.

Lucas let her go and pinned Roderick with a stare that said, Try me.

"Stop it. Both of you!" Saffron cried out.

"Roderick, darling, the hot water ran out, as you well know." Saffron looked at him beseechingly, pleading with him to get her meaning.

"Sorry, I forgot, sweetheart." Roderick walked with a possessive air and kissed her full on the mouth and gave her a slap on her bum, before showing Lucas the door.

"We don't want you here, mate," Roderick said coldly. Saffron had never seen him act so masculine.

Lucas looked Saffron over and cast a derisive glance around the room before leaving.

Saffron stayed where she was, trembling until Roderick came back inside and hugged her.

She fell to pieces. Roderick wrapped an arm around her shoulders and guided her to the sofa. After gentle prodding, she told him everything.

"You know he'll be back," Roderick said.

She nodded. "But why is he here now? After all this time?"

Roderick shrugged. "Maybe he just found out where you live or something?"

Saffron frowned. "I don't think so. If he found me then he knows about the children. Oh my God, he's come to take the children!" she exclaimed.

"Let's not jump to conclusions. If he wanted the children, he would have taken them a long time ago," Roderick said. "So don't jump the gun. Let me give Jefferson a ring. He's one of the best solicitors I know. We'll have Lucas wrapped in so much legal red tape by tomorrow he won't know what hit him. Saffron, believe me. He won't get the children."

Saffron nodded, but still bit her lip.

"Now go and shower," Roderick ordered gently. "You smell a bit funky."

❧❧❧❧

For two long days, Saffron watched the road. She'd thought about going to Kingston for a few days but then decided she needed to get this over with. Lucas couldn't be so changed.

Roderick had left, promising to come back and visit before leaving for England in two weeks.

Saffron was at the far side of the house, using a long machete like a professional to dig up some yellow yams for dinner, when Lucas finally returned.

He stood with the sun behind him, wearing mirrored sunglasses, a navy pinstripe suit, a brilliant white silk shirt and a tie.

Saffron put the machete down and looked at him wearily.

"Are you alone?" Lucas asked eventually. He was having a hard time keeping his eyes away from the patch of sweat beneath each of her breasts and was thoroughly annoyed with himself when he felt his dick hardening.

"Alone, as in?"

"The boyfriend. Or is he the husband yet?" Lucas asked.

"He's gone. Temporarily." Jefferson had told her to give him at least three days to get the legal papers in place and to use Roderick just as they'd planned. "He'll be back soon."

"Where is the child?" Lucas asked.

Didn't he know there was more than one? Saffron thought. "Why would you want to know about my child?" she replied, trying to remain calm but feeling the bubble of panic roll around her stomach.

"Is there a reason why I shouldn't ask about it?"

"None whatsoever," she said, lifting her chin. "Taking its nap."

Lucas nodded. Waiting.

"How old is it?" he asked, watching the way she tapped the machete against her boot nervously. Was she so promiscuous she didn't know the kid's father? And why was she so nervous?

"Look, why are you here, Lucas?" Saffron asked, losing patience.

"I was buying that plot of land at the beach when your name came up," he replied. "Tell them to sell it to me, Saffron."

She planted her hands on her hips.

"Or what? You're going to smack my bottom and tie me up!"

"We had done many things together, Saffron, but not that. But then I'll try anything once," he answered flicking a glance at her breasts. "Did we make a baby that night, Saffron?" he asked suddenly.

"No, we did not!" she answered quickly, because they really didn't on the night he was referring to. The twins were conceived much later in his office.

"And you would tell me?" He took one step and then another until he was within the shade of the numerous yam vines and only inches away from touching her. "Wouldn't you, Saffron?"

He ran a finger down her neck and watched intently as it slid into the little dip at her collar bone.

She stepped back.

"Not that night, Lucas," she reiterated sternly.

He came forward again. He couldn't help himself. She was dressed in mud-stained shorts that reached her knees and a thin orange top soaked with sweat. He should have been turned off, yet here she was with mud in her finger nails, a tasteless straw hat with a huge bunch of straw flowers on it and workman boots that looked too big for her.

"Don't come any closer," Saffron warned when he reached out to touch her again. She lifted the machete defensively.

He smiled, and just as he was about to wrestle it from her, he was knocked to the ground by a large, angry man wielding a sword and a huge horse.

"What the hell!" Lucas bellowed from the wet ground before rising furiously.

Suddenly, two men dressed in dark suits and sunglasses came charging around the house and put Mas Arthur in a head lock before Saffron realized what was happening.

"Call them off!" she screamed. "Call them off!" She lunged for the men, grabbing one by the hair and yanking as hard as she could before the other lifted her off the ground.

"Take your hands off her," Lucas ordered and Saffron found herself being lowered to the ground again. She threw a punch and hit the man who had grabbed her before going after the other man who was holding Mas Arthur.

"Let him go," Lucas ordered, seeing the frail old man he had thought was a lot younger. The horse was in fact an old donkey that looked like it belonged in a museum.

Lucas blushed, a feeling he had not felt in a very long time. But to give them credit, his security guards had acted instinctively. He was a very wealthy man and had inherited all of his father's enemies. So seeing a threat they had taken action.

Saffron went straight to Mas Arthur, who was looking pale, and hugged him.

"Are you all right?" she asked with tears in her eyes.

Mas Arthur could only nod. Saffron turned to Lucas and gave him a filthy, accusing look. "Get off my property," she ordered. "And take them with you." She nodded towards the other two men in suits. One she recognized from the night in the coffee bar with Lucas's father.

Turning her back on them, she walked Mas Arthur inside and sat him down on the sofa. Only after hearing the car drive away did she finally relax.

కూడ్ఆ

"I want to see my child!" a voice shouted.

Saffron looked up, startled to see Lucas looming over her with papers in his hand. She had been feeding the chickens and dodging Matilda the over-protective mother hen.

"Child, Lucas?"

"You lied to me!"

"I did no such thing!"

"I asked you if you had conceived that night, and what did you tell me?"

"But I didn't conceive that night. It was almost a month later in your office!" Saffron said.

The silence which greeted her confession was deafening.

Lucas looked a little like his normal self. He was without the suit jacket, but the tie was very much in place, as were the sunglasses.

He raked an unsteady hand through his short hair and then removed his sunglasses. The look he sent her way made Saffron wish he would put them back on, but she knew him well enough to know when he was struggling with his emotions.

Legally, he couldn't come near her and the children. Jefferson had been that fast and thorough, giving her leverage against his millions, power and influence.

"Would you like a glass of water?" Saffron asked softly and walked indoors.

It was cool inside, and after taking out two brightly coloured plastic cups, she poured them both some water.

"Twins," she said eventually, breaking the silence.

"Excuse me?"

"I had twins. A boy and a girl. Bella is such a tomboy right now; it's like having two boys," Saffron joked.

Lucas stared at her with a vacant expression.

"They're sleeping at the moment, thankfully," she said. "They wake up at five and are on the go until lunch time, then they crash for a couple of hours."

Lucas said nothing. He just looked at her in a way that made her feel very small.

"Come." She took his hand and pulled him to the children's room.

They were sleeping like little angels. Saffron already knew they looked like Lucas, his strong Italian genes dominating her Jamaican ones. Both children had the blackest soft hair, which curled adoringly. Their eyes were the exact shade of their father's. Their skin was a soft golden brown.

Saffron turned to look at Lucas. He had turned very pale and just stared down at the twins, his face unreadable, but the grip with which he held her hand was revealing.

Suddenly he looked up. "You lied to me again, Saffron," he said menacingly, his golden eyes flashing with something close to hate. "You lied and took my children."

He turned away from her and walked out of the room. Saffron grabbed him to prevent him from going to the front door.

"I didn't lie," she pleaded.

"You never told me. Or didn't you know who the father was?"

She slapped him, a stinging blow that vibrated around the room.

Lucas grabbed her shoulders and hauled her to him.

"One, two, three times and you're out, Saffron," he said, his tawny eyes darkening.

His mouth quickly stormed hers, and she turned away to deny him access. But then he sank his mouth to her neck instead, running his warm tongue along her skin, causing her to whimper and her nipples to harden. In seconds his mouth came back to hers and she was kissing him back with a hunger that had not been fed for a very long time.

He laid her down on the sofa, pulling her strap down her arm so he could suck on her plump brown nipple. Saffron whimpered in pleasure. Moving quickly, he unfastened her shorts and had them down to her knees when the first cry stopped Saffron from reaching for his erect member.

"Lucas, no," she said.

"Lucas, yes," he whispered against the softness of her stomach. "That's what you should be saying," he added before twirling his tongue into her belly button.

"No! Lucas, the children are waking!"

Saffron finally got through to him, and he swiftly moved away from her, turning his back and going out to the verandah.

Saffron adjusted her clothes and went to get Bella before Nico woke up.

By the time she came back to the living room Lucas had left.

⁂

Lucas stood on the verandah, gripping the railing tightly and looking out at the view. He'd been around Saffron for three days and already he was an emotional wreck.

Saffron did things to him and said things that only she could get away with. He resented the way she made him feel.

Lucas felt a tightness in the pit of his stomach, and it was rapidly rising, choking him. He had to get out of here. He needed to go, but before he thought about himself he had to think about the children. He needed to get on the phone to Dean, his solicitor, immediately. He had a will to change, his twins' future to secure should anything happen to him.

Lucas groaned and rubbed his hands over his face. He wanted to go inside and look at them again. Touch them and wake them up. They had looked so small in that cot, dressed in only nappies.

Why were they sleeping in one bed? he asked himself, frowning. Was Saffron so hard-pressed for money that she could only afford one cot? Did she hate him so much that she couldn't come to him for help? But even if she did hate him, she had deprived his children of a father and the comfort and security only he could provide. And what was Roderick doing here again? Where did he factor into all of this? *I'll be damned if I will sit back and watch another man raise my children. Saffron may hate me, but she'll be brought to heel!*

❧◦❧❧◦❧

Saffron changed Bella into a clean nappy. She used the type made from old fashioned cloth, as both babies had had allergic reactions to the modern disposable ones. Though cloth nappies were cheaper, washing them never seemed to end.

Carrying Bella into the living room, Saffron spied Lucas through the screen door and went reluctantly out to him. Bella had her fingers in her mouth as she always did when she was still sleepy, with her head on Saffron's shoulder.

Lucas was on his mobile phone, talking rapidly in what sounded like Italian. She didn't even know he spoke Italian.

Saffron reached out and touched his shirt sleeve. Lucas spun around, ready to do battle, but instantly froze, seeing his daughter's golden gaze on him for the first time.

"This is Isabella," Saffron said. "But I call her Bella."

Lucas stared. He knew he was supposed to do something, say something, but he had never seen a baby up close in his life before, and this one was watching him with eyes the exact shade as his. Bella held a chubby arm out to him.

"She wants to go to you," Saffron said, tears running down her face.

Lucas swallowed nervously and gently took his daughter. The child smelled of sweet, generous innocence. Bella put her head on his shoulder and wrapped a tiny arm around his neck. They sighed together.

With his throat tight with emotion, Lucas turned to Saffron, his eyes blazing. "You bitch," he said before turning away.

Saffron turned into the house with a stricken gasp. She went into her bedroom and flung herself onto the bed to cry. Things would change now; she saw the promise of it in his eyes. He was not about to go away, and the world as she knew it was probably over.

Lucas went in search of Saffron sometime later. Bella was babbling away, and his shirt sleeve was damp. Saffron couldn't even afford proper nappies, Lucas thought, feeling angry.

He found her face down on the bed.

"She is wet," he said, glancing around the room. The bed was made of wood with a simple white mosquito net suspended from the ceiling. The room was simply furnished. Lucas's mouth tightened; he was not impressed by the sparseness.

"I'll take her." Saffron sat up and wiped her eyes with her fingers before taking the baby from Lucas. But Bella had other ideas. She didn't want to let him go and a slight tug of war ensued.

"No, no, no, no," Bella cried, screaming her favourite word.

"Come on, darling. Daddy will be right here," Saffron coaxed.

"Sit on the bed," Saffron ordered Lucas.

"Excuse me?"

"She won't let me change her if she can't see you," Saffron explained. "Sit on the bed."

Lucas sat and watched, fascinated as Saffron quickly changed his daughter into another cloth nappy, securing it with pins.

Bella cooed at him and he scooped her up confidently when she was clean and fresh. He was about to take her outside again when he heard a cry from the bedroom next door.

"Come on, Bella, take me to your brother."

"His name is Nico," Saffron interjected. She knew she wasn't welcome and stepped back when Lucas threw a hostile look in her direction.

"Come, Bella, you introduce Daddy to Nico," he said. He went into the other room, closing the door behind him.

❧❧❧❧

Lucas looked after the twins while Saffron made a simple dinner of roast breadfruit and saltfish. The breadfruit she roasted on a small fire outside to save her cooking gas. Lucas carried both children with ease, talking to them in soft Italian while walking around the house and gardens. For a brief moment of panic, Saffron thought he was about to take them away when she couldn't see them. She ran around the house only to stop short upon seeing him talking and shaking hands with Mas Arthur.

As if feeling her eyes on him, Lucas suddenly turned to look at her. She knew that he knew what she had been thinking, and she blushed guiltily before shamefully walking away.

Lucas didn't talk to her at all through dinner, giving his children all his attention, and for a moment Saffron felt jealous.

After bath and a story, the children were put to bed. Saffron, ignoring Lucas who was now on his phone again, went to take a shower, hoping he would have left by the time she came out. No such luck. Dressed in another pair of shorts and a top and wearing mosquito repellant, Saffron reluctantly went into the living room.

"Is this where you say we need to talk," she asked, desperately hoping to lighten the mood.

Lucas looked her over with hostile eyes. "No, this is where I talk and you listen. I am leaving in three days."

"And this matters to me because?"

His eyes flashed with annoyance.

"Why do you always do it?" he asked softly.

"Do what?"

"Like to live dangerously."

Saffron put her hands on her hips and lifted her chin. "Maybe because you don't scare me," she said. "I knew you when you were real, when you were kind and supportive and not walking around with bodyguards and looking down your arrogant nose at us, lesser mortals. I can tell you now. I preferred you penniless!"

Lucas sighed. This was more like the Saffron he knew. She had been acting like a doormat all day and he'd hated it.

"When I leave, you come with me," he said.

"I don't think so."

"You think not?"

"You can forget it. This is our home."

"This glorified shed you dare to grow my children in?" he seethed.

"This is not a shed."

"You live in a wooden house with an open fireplace," he responded. "No proper locks on the doors or windows. My children dressed in nappies with pins sticking out of them! No proper lighting or drainage around the house. No fence for security. They could walk down to the road and be run over! And one cot!"

Saffron blanched with every accusation. He'd obviously spent all day collecting his inventory to hurl at her later.

"They sleep better in one cot," she defended.

"All sorts of men coming and going—"

"Excuse me, the only men coming here are you, Mas Arthur and Roderick," Saffron said.

"Myself and Mas Arthur are not included. In fact, I have much to be grateful to the old man for," he said. "But let me see that money-grabbing degenerate around my children again, and you will live to regret it!"

Saffron was dumbfounded.

"He's my friend, and it's not pins in the nappies, it's safety pins!" she exclaimed

"Whatever." Lucas threw up his hands in a dismissive gesture. "I was your friend and you screwed me! He's gone, and I mean it."

Saffron drew in a deep breath. "Just who the hell do you think you are coming in here and ordering me about, telling me who can or can't visit me?" Saffron asked.

Lucas towered over her. "I am the man who fathered those children. Children you deprived me of." His eyes flashed with anger. "What did I ever do to you to deserve that kind of treatment?"

Saffron sobbed.

"And don't you dare start crying until I'm finished!" Lucas snarled.

He was so angry, Saffron could literally see it coming off him in waves.

"We are going back to England."

"No, I'm staying here," replied Saffron.

"Fine. Then you stay, but the children come with me."

"No. You can't take the children!"

"I can and I will," Lucas replied. "You deprived me of their first year of life, and you will pay Saffron. You will pay."

Lucas stood straight and unshakable, his mouth flattened to a line.

"You're not like this," Saffron whispered through her tears. "Threatening people to get what you want." She lifted her chin. "I've got papers, keeping the twins with me. You'll have to take me to court to even get access. I can—"

Lucas laughed harshly. "That's where you're wrong, sweetheart." He walked towards her, circling her slowly. "One thing you can't afford to be when dealing with me, Saffron," he said, "is to be complacent. Your solicitors overlooked a major factor."

"No, they didn't," Saffron said.

"We have twins, Saffron. Twins. If you had bothered to look at the papers it clearly states one female child."

She was shocked. It couldn't be true. How could Roderick not tell Jefferson she had twins!

"That's right, Saffron," he said, seeing her shock and revelling in it. "I will take one child. It's better to have one for now until I get the other, and I promise you, no judge on earth would leave a child with you after all that I've seen."

Saffron swayed in distress. It was all too much for her. He wouldn't take her babies from her, he just wouldn't. She reached out a pleading hand to him, which he ignored. She struggled to catch her breath and keep the light-headed feeling at bay. She failed.

∾∾∾∾

"If you think you can impress me with your little fainting charade you have another thing coming," Lucas said a few minutes later when she eventfully revived. Saffron was lying on the sofa, and he was kneeling down on the rug beside her, his face close to hers.

She closed her eyes again.

"Go away," she whispered, feeling sick.

"If I go, the children come with me," he said. "Where are you going?" he asked as she pushed past him and ran to the bathroom to throw up.

Lucas went with her, wiping her forehead with a damp cloth and holding her hair away from her face until she finished.

"Here." He'd put toothpaste on her toothbrush.

She snatched the toothbrush from him, brushed her teeth and washed her face as he watched her silently.

"I'm going to bed," Saffron said. He followed her into the bedroom. She swung around to face him.

"Don't worry," Lucas said. "Seeing you dressed as a farmer is a total turn-off. As you know, I like my women perfumed and powdered and preferably blonde."

"Why do you hate me so much?" Saffron asked and grabbed the hem of her top, hauled it over her head and shimmied out of her shorts within seconds.

Her naked breasts bounced as she grabbed the plain white t-shirt she kept under her pillow and put it on. Lucas watched her intently. Her body was still as beautiful, if not more so, since the birth. Her breasts were fuller, the sweep of her hips wider and her stomach soft and round.

"I loved you once, Saffron," he said, his golden gaze capturing hers as she slid between the covers. "But you played me like a fool. It will never happen again."

They were silent, the only sound coming from the insects calling to each other outside.

Lucas turned to go.

"I never lied to you, Lucas," Saffron said softly.

He stopped and turned to look at her. "It doesn't matter now, does it, Saffron?"

"Yes, it does." She sat up and hugged her knees to her chest, "You're punishing me—"

"Don't you think I have a right to punish you?" He turned to go and she quickly reached out and grabbed his arm.

"Listen to me!" she said. "The first time I saw Roderick was after we made love, Lucas. Not before. After. He was in England, and I didn't know."

Lucas stared at her, his face hard and unreadable.

"As I said before, it doesn't matter now," he said, pulling away. "I'll sleep in the spare room. I don't trust you not to bolt with my children again."

Chapter Six

Lucas walked out onto the verandah. The night was warm. Slowly, he undid his tie. He was so used to wearing it nowadays, it was no longer the noose it once felt like.

What a day, he thought, looking out into the darkness. There was nothing to see but never-ending blackness. It was like facing his own gloomy thoughts, so he went back inside the house.

At least the house was clean, he thought, looking around. A few toys in a basket in one corner, a bookcase in another but no television, he noticed for the first time. He couldn't even watch the news. This was beyond bloody basic, he thought in frustration. He went to have a shower.

Lucas couldn't sleep. The bed was hard and narrow, and he longed for the massive king-sized bed and huge pillows at the house he had rented further along the coast, near Port Antonio.

Sitting up, he shoved the flat single pillow behind his head. Saffron had looked so different, he thought. She was still beautiful but in a more womanly way. Motherhood had certainly brought out her beauty and she seemed more comfortable in her skin.

Years ago, she wouldn't dare go out without a touch of lipstick, and her hair had always been immaculate in long extensions. Lucas smiled in the darkness.

He knew he had to move past the bitterness and anger now that he had children to think about. Bella, his beautiful daughter with her quick smile and constant babbling, and Nico, who was a little more serious. Lucas loved his kids. He would be the best father, and his first move would be to have them fed and properly clothed.

Reaching for his phone, Lucas rang Muzio. There was no way he was going to sleep tonight. Wearing his black silk boxers, he unlocked the front door to sit outside and wait.

࿇

Saffron woke with a start and dashed out of bed to check on the children. She relaxed when she saw that they were sleeping peacefully.

She heard a grunting noise outside and walked stealthily to the screen mesh. The front door was open, and she could see Lucas fighting another man. With a horrified gasp, she realised it was the same man who had beat him up that night in the coffee bar all those years ago.

Without thinking, Saffron charged at the man and jumped onto his back, pulling his hair as she tried to throw him to the ground. "You leave him alone!" she screamed, raking her fingernails down the side of his face. He groaned, and with a skilful twist, he pinned her to the cold ground with his knee pressed in her stomach.

"Leave her, Muzio!" Lucas ordered.

Muzio released Saffron and offered a hand to help her up. Saffron ignored it. Muzio went to the car to get two white towels, handing one to Lucas before using one on himself. Both men watched Saffron in silence.

"What's going on?" she asked. She wanted to go to Lucas to make sure he was all right, but he was watching her with a puzzled expression on his face.

"We were sparring, Saffron," Lucas said, hooking the towel around his neck while holding both ends.

Saffron looked from one man to the other. They both had on similar baggy trousers and were barefooted. Lucas was bare-chested while the other man wore a simple vest.

"He wasn't hurting you?" she asked, whispering.

"We were fighting. I asked him for a fight."

"But I thought..." It was all too much for Saffron. Sobbing, she dashed into the house.

Lucas went after her, bidding Muzio a hurried good-night. He grabbed the lamp, extinguished it and locked the front door.

"Hey," Lucas whispered, standing at Saffron's bedroom door.

"Go away," she mumbled from under a pillow.

Lucas went in, closed the door and walked over to her bed. He pulled the mosquito net over his head and sat beside her.

"I'm sorry, Saff," he said gently. "I didn't mean to frighten you." She mumbled something he didn't quite catch and grabbed the pillow off her head.

She was crying but this time her tears didn't annoy him.

"I thought he was hurting you like he did that night," Saffron said, her voice shaking with emotion.

He put a finger to her cheek. "Muzio was the only friend I had growing up in my father's house," Lucas said. "My mother had been banished to Scotland, and I hardly saw her. Muzio was the only one who dared to befriend me."

"But he would have killed you that night."

"No. His loyalty was to my father, but he wasn't touching me. He only made it look as though he was."

"And tonight I know what I saw. I saw him kick you in the stomach."

"We were sparring. You should have seen me knock him to the ground before you came out. You would have been proud of me," he bragged. "I couldn't sleep, Saff, so I called him over."

"I don't like seeing you fight like that. You could get hurt."

"You were sensational though," said Lucas.

"I think I scratched him."

Lucas laughed. "He will wear you marks with pride."

"How can you say that?"

"You fought him to save me. No one but him has ever done that before, Saff."

"You are the twin's dad."

"No. It's more than that. Isn't it, Saffron?" Lucas asked.

"No."

"Yes."

He leaned over and kissed her. A warm tender kiss that sparked a flame of remembrance within her.

"You should not have done that, Lucas," Saffron said.

"Why?"

"We are enemies and you're going to take th—"

Lucas didn't let her finish. He kissed her again, a little longer this time, familiarising himself with the shape of her mouth.

Lucas ran his tongue around her ear lobe, dipping into the shell before sucking it tenderly and moving on to the other ear. Each little kiss, each nip of his strong teeth and touch of his warm tongue was a sensual surprise for Saffron.

Lucas loved the softness of Saffron's body. Her breasts fit into his hands perfectly. He explored her belly button and grazed her stomach with his teeth, moving her feet apart to kiss her between her legs.

Saffron was on the brink of orgasm, crying and clawing and begging him to release her. He moved slowly, kissing his way up to her mouth, as she sweated and trembled with each touch.

She screamed when he finally entered her with a slow, powerful thrust. She grabbed his body, grinding against him, but Lucas wouldn't let her set the pace. His thrusts were deep and measured, and she moved until she could touch his bum to urge him on.

"Please," she begged.

"Is this what you want, sweetheart?"

"Yes."

"Not yet." He withdrew and moved downwards, kissing her quivering thighs and the back of her knees. She knew him well enough to know that this was a power play. He always did it, trying to manipulate her. But, for once, this game she would play and win.

Abruptly, she sat up and reversed their positions.

Sitting across his hard thighs, she leaned forward and kissed him deeply. She kissed his shoulders, sucked on his flat nipples and followed the trail of hair down his chest until she reached his waist.

The smooth tip of his penis nudged against her mouth, and she kissed it before trailing and blowing against the long, hard length of it.

Lucas felt himself losing control. No other woman had ever done what Saffron was doing to him.

With a quick movement Lucas flipped her onto her back and slipped inside her. He moved urgently, and she raised her hips to meet each rapid thrust.

She couldn't get enough. The pleasure was intense.

Lifting her legs until they were over his shoulders, Lucas surged into her, groaning with pleasure until she screamed his name and bit his shoulders. Her muscles clenched thightly around him, drawing everything from him, and with one last thrust he ejaculated inside her.

They stayed joined together, breathing hard for some time until Lucas, aware of his weight, moved off Saffron and pulled her to his side. They fell asleep, exhausted, with her bottom pressed against him and his hand on her breast.

⚜

Saffron opened her eyes at the first cry of one of the children. Usually it was Nico who woke first, and she would have to pick him up and take him back to her bed until Bella woke, normally about half an hour later.

But as Saffron groggily tried to get up, she realised she couldn't move her legs as they were pinned to the bed by something warm and heavy. Saffron opened her eyes fully, only to see Lucas fast asleep beside her.

She could not believe that she had had sex with him last night. Tugging her legs free, she groped around on the floor, looking for her t-shirt. Another cry from the other room made her hurry. Two babies waking and demanding breakfast at the same time was a little daunting for her. She was not a morning person.

Saffron picked up her son with his blanket, and he greeted her with a huge smile and smacked his lips to her cheek with a wet kiss. Cuddling her son, Saffron went into the kitchen to fetch a bottle of thin cornmeal porridge from the fridge. Nico liked his porridge cold. Bella liked hers warm.

Saffron lay on the sofa and cuddled Nico as he drank his porridge greedily. If she was lucky, he just might fall asleep again.

Lucas looked around for several seconds until he remembered where he was. He could not believe he slept with Saffron again.

Where was she anyway? he asked himself, pulling on his trousers. He couldn't find his shirt. He went to look for Saffron.

He found her asleep in the living room with both children by her side, sleeping too. Two almost empty bottles of yellow grainy stuff were on the small table beside them.

Lucas looked at his family tenderly, before going into the bathroom, to have a quick shower and then get dressed. He felt great. Sex with Saffron always took a lot out of him, but he usually felt rewarded ten fold afterwards. He had never felt this satisfied and relaxed in his life.

Saffron and the kids were awake by the time he finished his shower. The children looked up and each gave him a grin. Bella jumped up and down on her mother's tummy excitedly.

"Good morning," Lucas said to them, lifting Nico and then Bella just as she was about to protest. He kissed them on the cheek and held them close.

"Can you look after them while I shower please?" Saffron asked shyly, avoiding Lucas's stare. She didn't know what to say.

"They've been fed, washed and changed, so they aren't hungry or anything," she said.

"You don't need to ask, Saffron, I am their father. Of course, I can look after them. Can't I, Nico? Daddy is going to take you for a morning stroll while mummy takes a nice long shower."

Saffron watched as Lucas playfully nibbled Nico's ear and then Bella's. The children squealed in delight.

Saffron showered quickly, dressed in a pair of beige shorts, flip flops and a white vest. She ruffled her hair and for a quick second thought about putting on some lipstick. She didn't bother.

Lucas was in the kitchen looking through her cupboards. He was not pleased with what he saw. The children were playing on the floor.

"I've only got cereal, Lucas," Saffron said, remembering the huge breakfasts Lucas always liked.

"Get the children ready. We're going," he replied, slamming the last cupboard door.

"Going where?"

"To my house.

"I told you last night, neither me or the children will be leaving Jamaica," Saffron said, picking up the children and holding them protectively.

Lucas's eyes flashed a white gold.

"And don't you think that looking at me like that will change my mind!" Saffron said. "You can't intimidate me!"

"I said nothing about leaving Jamaica, Saffron. I simply meant, if you had let me finish, that we go to the house I rented in Port Antonio."

"Oh," she said with relief. "Why?"

He threw his hands in the air impatiently. "I want food. I want a hot shower and I want..." Lucas' eyes darkened, and he looked directly at her breasts.

"You want?"

"Sex," he said. "But, Saffron, don't be thinking anything has changed."

"Why would I think that?"

"After last night."

"You came to my room, Lucas. Not the other way round."

"I'm still going back to England with the children whether you come or not."

"I don't think so," Saffron shot back.

Lucas walked over and plucked the children from her arms.

Saffron gasped and tried to grab them back.

"You've got five minutes," he said, walking into the living room and sitting on the sofa, bouncing the children on each knee.

"Four minutes," he warned, seeing Saffron still standing in the doorway, biting her lips in indecision.

Saffron flew into the children's room and gathered up their baby bags, stuffing them with everything she could get her hands on.

"We're going to the car," Lucas called out a short while later.

She knew he would leave her if she let him. There was no way he was taking the twins out without her. He could disappear with them, Saffron thought.

She locked up the place and dashed outside.

Lucas was waiting impatiently by his Jeep, the children clutching his trouser legs.

"Have you got car seats?" she asked as she was about to open the back door.

Looking into the Jeep and seeing no car seats, Saffron slammed the door shut.

"We'll take my car," she said.

He looked at her little car that looked like something Nico could play with.

"I think not. Here, hold these two while I get the car seats from that thing." He walked away, quickly swinging back. "How can you drive around in that small thing with my children!"

"There is nothing wrong with my car," Saffron said.

"There is everything wrong with it. My children deserve better, and I am disgusted that you would think they deserve less than the very best."

Saffron gasped. With her back stiffened, she waited for him to secure the car seats in his car.

"Saffron?" Lucas said as they drove off.

Saffron turned to look at him wearily.

"I'm sorry for what I said."

"No, you're not," she replied.

He breathed in deeply, as the car moved onto the main road.

"Ok, I'm not, but I don't want to fight with you, especially in front of the twins."

"Oh, we will fight, Lucas," Saffron said, "as there is no way in hell I am letting you take my children from me."

He slammed on the brakes and pulled off the road in anger. The driver behind them blew his horn loudly as he swerved to avoid hitting them from behind.

"Why did you do that!" Saffron shouted, glaring at Lucas. "What kind of reckless driving is that? The children are in the car for God's sake," she added, turning to make sure the kids were fine. Nico's cheeks looked a little flushed, but both children were still asleep.

"It was reflex," Lucas said.

"That's not good enough. The children are in the car, and I expect you to drive slowly and carefully!"

"You've had a whole year and a half to get this parenting thing together. I've only had a day!"

"But still—"

"But nothing. I'm sorry, okay. They're fine. You're fine. The whole damn island is fine!" he shouted.

"Don't you shout at me," Saffron said.

Lucas threw his hands in the air and was about to drive off, then changed his mind. He grabbed Saffron's head to face him and kissed her roughly.

She pushed his shoulders to get away, but he wouldn't let her go. Instead he forced his tongue into her mouth. She bit it.

"Bitch," Lucas mumbled before deepening his kiss. He lifted her top and put her left nipple into his mouth until she moaned his name.

"Truce," Lucas said.

"What?" she whispered, caressing his head.

"Truce," he repeated.

"Truce, Lucas."

"Good." He quickly moved to the other nipple, licked and sucked it deeply and then kissed her lips. He looked into her eyes and smiled.

Saffron smiled back as he started the Jeep and moved onto the road again. The day was bright and promising.

❧❦❧❦

They were each holding a sleepy twin when Lucas opened the door to a large house off the main road, it's entrance hidden by large, waxy crotons and pink-flowered oleanders. Saffron had driven on this road a thousand times but had never noticed the property.

The house was painted in a soft coral hue and looked attractive with its white shutters and doors and wide cobbled driveway.

"Who owns it?" Saffron asked, looking around at the neat gardens. She could hear the heavy roar of the waves and looked in that direction, not realising they were close to the beach. She could see a yacht tied to a short pier behind the house.

"A banking friend," Lucas said. He couldn't wait to find Muzio, have him look after the twins for an hour while he took Saffron to bed. Breakfast could wait, he had another appetite that needed satisfaction first.

"Nobody I would know then," Saffron said wearily.

"No, Saffron," Lucas said. "Nobody you would know." He kissed her before pushing open the door.

"Surprise!" a female voice shouted from inside. Lucas froze.

Saffron looked around to see a diminutive blonde dressed in only a red ribbon and posing provocatively with her arms over her head, her back arched and her big, fake-looking boobs thrust high in the air.

"Oh, I didn't know you had visitors, Gianluca?" the blonde said, slowly lowering her arms but making no attempt to cover herself.

"Rebecca," Lucas growled, "what are you doing here?"

"You forgot to invite me, so I thought I'd come along and keep you company."

"I'll get Muzio to take you back to the airport," Lucas said.

"But—what's that?" the blonde asked.

Lucas didn't know what she was talking about. "What?" he asked impatiently.

Rebecca pointed at Bella, who was snuggled into Lucas's shoulder. "That."

Saffron had had enough. Lucas was actually having a conversation with a naked woman, whom he was obviously on intimate terms with. She was okay with that, but no one was going to insult her children.

"That is his daughter, and this is his son," Saffron said, stepping past Lucas and throwing him a scathing look. "I need to put him down," she added, referring to Nico, who was getting warm.

Lucas pointed down a long corridor. "Any room will do. Come back and get Bella."

Saffron set her son gently on the bed and shielded him with pillows before going to get her daughter.

Lucas showed Rebecca into the pool house after she begged him to let her stay for a little holiday now that she was already in Jamaica. Technically, as she had pointed out, she was still his girlfriend until he gave her a parting gift. The tears in her eyes quickly dried when he told her he'd let her stay and give her an extra present for being understanding.

Lucas left her unpacking her things and returned to main house.

He went into his makeshift office to ring his mother, knowing he was about to make her the happiest women on the planet.

⇛⇛⇝⇝

The twins were still asleep when Saffron went to check on them. She lay close to Nico, watching him sleep, knowing he was better left undisturbed.

Saffron spent the next few minutes thinking about the huge assumption she had made. Lucas was a wealthy, highly-sexed and good looking man, but for her own self respect, she had to set some boundaries. Every time they were alone they practically fell on each other. But Lucas was not exclusive. She had to remember that. She was tall and skinny with small breasts and stretch marks on her stomach. She was not his ideal woman. He'd told her so yesterday. But he had loved her once.

She sighed again, looking around the room. It was air-conditioned and painted in cool blues, but it looked like any other room rich people supplied for their guests. Every comfort, but no comfort at all.

Twenty minutes later Saffron was desperately trying to calm Nico. He was crying inconsolably. His long eyelashes were stuck together with tears as he looked at his mother to make him better. But she had nothing to give him. No Calpol or teething gel, not even his toy elephant.

Bella woke and started to cry too. Almost in tears herself, Saffron picked them both up and went in search of Lucas. She couldn't find him but saw the keys to the Jeep on a side table and quickly secured the crying children in their seats and drove off.

⇛⇛⇝⇝

Saffron always took the children to the Port Antonio hospital as it was easy to reach and not overcrowded with tourists. She didn't wait long this time and was walking out of the doctor's office with a prescription for baby ibuprofen and ear drops for Nico when she saw Lucas striding down the corridor towards her.

"Why didn't you get me!" he shouted, his face dark with rage.

Saffron ignored him. "Thanks for all the help, Nurse Green," she said to the nurse, a friend, who was holding Bella.

"No problem, Miss Saffron. You just take this little one home. Me never see him so sick before," Nurse Green said.

"That's Lucas, the dad." Saffron said.

Nurse Green looked him over and kissed her teeth. "Here," she said and handed Bella to him. "Me not impressed with you, young man. Leaving a mother to look after two babies by herself is not right. Not right, I tell you. But we look after her and the pickney dem. We look after our own."

Lucas's gold eyes darkened. Saffron thought he was about to explode, but he said nothing, standing stiffly under the barrage of accusations from Nurse Green.

"Thanks again, Nurse Green. See you in church," Saffron said and hurriedly turned away.

Saffron quickly strode down the long corridor, aware of Lucas's anger. She didn't care. Nico's temperature had gone down a little. Saffron went to the pharmacy to fill the prescription, turning to Lucas a moment later.

"I'm really sorry, Lucas. I left my purse," she said nervously. His silence was telling. "Could you lend me some money to pay for this until w—"

Saffron was cut off by the slashing of his hand through the air, and she quickly stepped back to let him pay for the medication. She then walked outside to the Jeep, which she had parked under a poinciana tree, leaving the doors wide open.

"I'm sorry. I was in a hurry," she said, looking at Lucas.

He said nothing.

"How did you get here anyway?" Saffron asked as she strapped Nico into the car seat from one side while Lucas secured Bella from the other.

"Muzio saw you leave," Lucas said.

Saffron stood at the driver's side with the keys in her hand. Lucas plucked them from her, grabbed her elbow and marched her around to the passenger side, where she resisted, bracing her hands on either side of the door.

"I don't—"

"Get in the car, Saffron," Lucas said. He then picked her up and practically threw her in the seat and slammed the door before she could object. Lucas drove them to the house in silence.

A huge delivery van was unpacking furniture when they reached the house.

"Baby stuff," Lucas said, referring to the furniture.

"We aren't staying," Saffron replied, going into the house ahead of him and walking past two men carrying an over-the-top toddler bed with rails into a room. The children weren't ready for a toddler bed yet, Saffron thought, shaking her head.

Lucas breathed in and then out slowly. He was frustrated. He pulled out his mobile phone, said a few words in Italian and Muzio appeared a short while later.

"Watch the children," Lucas ordered. He grabbed Saffron's arm, pulling her out of the bedroom, down the hall and into his bedroom, and slammed the door shut.

"How dare you leave my house with my children and not tell me!"

"There was no time to go off looking for you. My children come first! And Nico was running a temperature," Saffron said her hands on her hips and her hair bouncing around her face.

"You still should have got me!"

"You were busy with your girlfriend!"

"Ex-girlfriend, and that is beside the point."

Saffron crossed her arms over her chest and lifted her chin. She was tired and just wanted to be with her children.

"Oh yeah, how long has she been an ex? Ten minutes?" she said, watching as the guilt creeped up Lucas's neck. "My God, you're a piece of work. You slept with me last night, knowing you belong to somebody else!"

"I belong to no one," he growled. "She is—"

Saffron turned her back, not wanting him to see her hurt.

"You gave me five minutes to get their bags ready. I didn't have a thermometer. I didn't have any teething gel and no Calpol," she sobbed, flicking away a tear. She sat on the bed. "I don't even have enough nappies for them! I let them down. Nico will want his elephant soon and Bella her blankie, and I left them." Saffron cried into her hands. "I let you come along and order me about, upsetting our routine. And now the children are suffering."

Lucas stood frozen in front of her. Saffron could see the toes of his shiny brown leather brogues on the marble tiles.

"I wish you had never found us," she whispered.

"Ok," he muttered, kneeling down in front of her and pulling her hands away from her face. He had never seen her look so miserable. The time had come for a compromise. "Ok," he said again, clearing his throat.

Chapter Seven

"*What* the hell are you doing now?" Lucas asked, finally finding Saffron at the back of the house. She had been avoiding him all week, spending hours digging something up, planting something else or doing an endless round of errands for the neighbours.

Saffron was balancing a long thin stick, which was taller than the house, trying to pick ackee with it. She dropped the stick in fright at the sound of Lucas's voice, and it fell inches from his highly polished shoes.

"Now look what you made me do!" Saffron screamed, placing her hands on her hips. She'd been battling the ackee tree all morning and had only a handful of ackees to show for it. She wanted to cook ackee and saltfish for breakfast the next day.

"What were you doing?" Lucas asked.

"Trying to get those." Saffron pointed at the densely leafed tree laden with fruit.

She wasn't making eye contact, and it annoyed the hell out of him. "And what are those?" he queried.

"The same things you had for breakfast two days ago," Saffron replied.

"I thought they were scrambled eggs." Lucas remembered the yellow stuff on his plate, mixed with salted fish, onions and sweet peppers.

"Scrambled eggs?!" Saffron exclaimed, giggling. "That must have been the weirdest eggs you had ever tasted!" Tears streamed down her face as she looked at him and burst out laughing again. It was the first time he had heard her laugh since he'd been in Jamaica.

❧❦❧❦

Lucas slept in the spare room at Saffron's place without complaint. But the atmosphere between him and Saffron was fraught with tension since that disastrous first day at his house. Lucas had made no mention of going back to England, and Saffron was not about to bring up the subject.

"What happened to the coffee bar," Saffron asked out of the blue one day.

"I closed it down," Lucas answered.

"I'm sorry. That must have been hard for you."

Lucas's smile was more like a tight stretching of lips. "I couldn't be in two places at the same time, and the bar was more hands on. I had commitments elsewhere," he said.

Saffron picked up the bowl and walked closer to him.

"I am sorry," she said. She knew how much the bar had meant to him and what closing it must have cost him emotionally. "Are you happy?"

He looked past her to the goats tied to bushes just below Mas Arthur's house.

"I have money, I have homes in several countries," he said and shrugged. "And I have plenty of women."

Saffron quickly dipped her head.

"I'd better go inside." Saffron stepped past him and he grabbed her forearm. Some of the ackee fell to the ground. "Yes?" she asked.

His desire must have shown on his face as she pulled away with a simple shake of her head and walked away. Lucas watched her go and then picked up the three ackee pods at his feet and followed her inside.

"How do you cook these then?" he asked.

Saffron turned to face him.

"Haven't you got something to do? Go bury your head in paperwork or something," she said.

"Anyone would think you don't want me here," he responded, his eyes narrowing.

"I don't."

"Tough. I'm here to stay."

Crossing her arms over her breasts, Saffron raised her chin.

"Since you are now Mr. International Business Man, there will be a time when you have to go. And I just can't wait for that day!"

"When I go, you come with me."

"We've been over this. This is our home and we're not leaving it." Saffron replied.

Lucas walked over and grabbed her waist, pressing her body against his.

"I will say this once. You and the children go where I go. I need to keep an eye on you."

"What! Don't be bloody ridiculous I'm not a five-year-old. I'm a grown woman!"

"Don't I know it," Lucas replied, spreading his hands on her firm buttocks and pressing her onto his aroused crotch. "But no one will ever touch you like this but me."

"Are you insane?" Saffron pressed her hands against his broad shoulders to look into his face.

"You are the mother of my children, and I expect you to adhere to certain principles."

"Don't talk rubbish," Saffron scoffed. "I may be a single mother, but I have no intention of ever staying single. Eventually, I will marry."

"You can't say that to me!"

"I can say whatever I bloody well please. I've told you before. You won't boss me around. You are their father, but that's it. Nothing else."

He moved her backwards until her back hit the wall.

"Nothing else, eh," he growled. Saffron pushed him away roughly.

"You stay away from me!" she shouted.

"Da da." A sleepy voice interrupted them from the doorway.

For a moment neither of them moved. Lucas shook his head gently as if to clear it. He looked tenderly down at his tiny daughter, who was rubbing her eyes sleepily from the doorway.

"Da da," Bella said again, lifting up her chubby arms to him.

Lucas scooped her up and cuddled her. It was the first time Bella had called him Daddy.

"Hiya, Gorgeous," Lucas said to his daughter, looking at Saffron over Bella's tiny shoulders. "How did she get out of the cot?" he asked.

"She must have climbed out," Saffron answered after a long pause. Frowning, she went into the children's bedroom. Nico was awake and must have seen his adventurous sister climb out as he was trying to do the same. "Oh no, sweetheart, that's naughty," Saffron said to her son, picking him up.

৯০০৫৬৯০০৫

Closing the door to the twins' room later in the day, Saffron went to the kitchen to get a glass of the ginger beer she had made earlier and a large wedge of bread and butter pudding. She took her snack out to the verandah.

It was blissfully quiet. Saffron sat down on the wrought iron chair, put her bare feet up on the railing and leaned back with a contented sigh to look out. A band of dark clouds gathered in the sky.

For once Saffron was alone, though Lucas had practically moved in, getting to know his twins. They knew him and accepted him, and like today when he wasn't around, they cried for him.

As the house was prone to power cuts and sudden electrical surges, Lucas did most of his work at his rented house. The hard drive on his laptop had been burnt out once already since being here and the signal on his mobile was poor.

He must be frustrated, Saffron thought, biting the corner of her bottom lip. This was living at it's simplest, but he never complained.

She forked a piece of pudding into her mouth, appreciating the way it melted on her tongue, and after sipping her drink she thought about the conversation that had precipitated a major change in Lucas almost a week ago.

They had driven from his rented house back to Saffron's in total silence. Bella had been awake and munching on a water cracker while Nico slept comfortably.

"Why do you use cloth nappies?" Lucas had asked. "I would have thought the disposable ones are more convenient."

"The first time I used them the twins had an allergic reaction," Saffron replied. "I had never been so frightened in my life, Lucas. Imagine, I'd only just got them home and had to take them back to the hospital again."

"I'm sorry."

"Why are you apologising?" Saffron asked.

"I'm sorry for not protecting you when I should have."

"To regret would be to deny their existence. I can't imagine life without them, but I was angry at first," Saffron admitted. "I had just started to sort myself out, making plans to open another shop like The Mother Lode here in Jamaica. I was about to sign a lease when I found out I was pregnant. It wasn't a good time for me."

"I'm really sorry, Saff," Lucas said. "Why didn't you tell me?"

She shrugged. "I couldn't get past your secretaries."

"You tried?"

Saffron turned to look at him bewildered. Did he really think she didn't want him to know about the pregnancy?

"Yes, of course I tried. You had every right to know about it, but then the pregnancy wasn't going so well, and I was put on bed rest," she said, shrugging again. "I had to concentrate on the babies."

Lucas's knuckles were stark white as he gripped the steering wheel. "How have you been managing?" he asked.

"I sold the shop and rented out the flat. Priorities change when you have children. They come first."

"Thank you, Saff," Lucas said a moment later, taking one hand off the steering wheel to hold one of hers. He lifted it to his lips and kissed her knuckles tenderly. And that was that.

Back on her verandah, Saffron watched as a doctor bird zoomed from one bright yellow hibiscus to the next. She tracked its frantic dash, wishing she had a camera.

The serenity was eventually broken as Lucas came up the hill in his black Jeep. Saffron watched him park beside her car under an almond tree, got out and walked towards her.

He was beautiful, she thought to herself, all lean muscle and broad shoulders. His hair had grown. He was wearing khaki chinos and a white polo shirt probably because she had teased him about his suits and ties. He looked tanned, healthy and relaxed. More like the Lucas she remembered.

"Hi," he said, reaching her and sitting in the chair beside hers.

"Hey. Finished everything?" Saffron asked. It had been like this for days, all politeness, and it was driving her insane.

"Yes, thank you," Lucas replied.

She could hear the buzz of the doctor bird as it flew closer.

"Where's the sidekick?" she asked.

Lucas looked at her with a puzzled frown.

"The sidekick? Muzio."

"He is not needed," Lucas said.

"Oh."

"I have some people coming to put up a fence."

Saffron, about to put a piece of pudding in her mouth, stopped and lifted an eyebrow at Lucas. Swiftly, he stood up and looked about, noticing the dense bushes where anyone could hide and the lack of outdoor lights. The place wasn't secure.

"I'm putting a discreet fence around the perimeter of this property too," he said.

"I don't think so," Saffron said.

"It has to be done."

"Why?"

"I thought that would be obvious."

"Not to me it isn't. I've lived here going on two years now. No one has come up here who wasn't supposed to come up here. I'm safe. We are a small community and—"

"You are a woman living alone with two very rich children," Lucas blurted.

"They don't need your money."

"Don't be ridiculous. It's their inheritance, and they won't be denied!"

Saffron stood up to face him with her hands on her hips.

"I can't believe you would burden them like that. Have you forgotten what your father tried to do to you? You're doing exactly the same thing!" she said.

"The fence and gate go up," Lucas reiterated, his mouth flattening to a thin white line.

"No! What about Mas Arthur? He uses my property to get to his."

"He will be given a pass."

"I guess you have it all figured out."

"You guess correctly."

"And what's with your speech. You never used to talk like that so bloody cold and arrogant!"

"You damned me to Hell once, Saffron. I think I'm living there now."

She flinched. "Why would you say such a thing?"

"I meet my children after almost two years. I live in this place—"

"You can leave any time you want," Saffron shouted with a toss of her head, indicating the direction of the road.

Lucas looked at her with disgust.

"I sleep on a lumpy bed with one pillow and I have no hot water!"

"Poor you," Saffron said.

"And every night I go to bed wanting to wake you up and sink myself inside you!"

"Sorry, I'm out of bounds. I won't be a convenient lay just because you feel the need for some physical release."

"You are the mother of my children," Lucas said.

"And that is exactly why you will continue to sleep in the spare room. We only have the children in common now, Lucas. You've changed and, well, I've changed for the better."

"I could change your mind."

"Don't you dare come any closer!" Saffron screeched, holding up her hands defensively when he took a step towards her.

"You could be pregnant already."

"Are you crazy?"

"It's true. I didn't use anything the other night."

"Are you usually so careless?"

"Only with you it seems," Lucas said with a rueful shrug. "Look."

Saffron looked at him. His hard-on was huge and straining against the zip of his trousers.

"How can you be so disgusting!"

He laughed, showing his perfectly white teeth, and stepped close enough to put his large hand against her soft stomach, spreading his fingers wide.

"Have we made another baby, Saffron?"

She knocked his hand away. "Two is enough."

"You should know I have an aunt who had several sets of multiples," he responded.

"Are you out of your mind!" Saffron exclaimed.

"I am. I am out of my mind with need. You need to wear a bra."

∾∾∾∾

A battered old car drove up to the house. Saffron stood up, ready to blast the driver for his tenacity, when the back door opened, and a tiny lady dressed in black with silver hair and dark, inquisitive eyes got out.

"Thank you," the lady said to the driver and paid him, before easing out a small leather travel bag and turning to Saffron with a brilliant smile.

"Hello. You must be Saffron Noble. May I introduce myself. Doratea Conti-Bridgewater," the lady said as she climbed the steps and sat down on a chair. "I know it's a bit of a shock, dear, but I've come to meet my grandbabies!"

Saffron didn't know how long she stood there as if frozen in place.

Doratea laughed. "Could I get a glass of water, please," she said, fanning herself with her hand, "It's been years since I've been in the Caribbean, and I'd forgotten how hot it actually is."

"I'm sorry. I--just I—" Saffron stammered.

The old lady laughed again. "That closed-mouthed son of mine is used to keeping a secret, but after he phoned the other night I had to come and meet the brave young lady who had my grandbabies all alone."

Saffron liked the woman's refreshing openness. After supplying Doratea with a cup of tea and a slice of pudding, they went to get the children, who were just waking.

∾∾∾∾

"Mother?" Lucas was bewildered upon spying his mother sitting in a shaded part of the garden with the children, singing nursery rhymes.

124

"Hello, son. Aren't you the proudest father ever? Say yeah for Daddy, children!" The kids clapped and cheered as they were instructed.

Lucas laughed, knelt down awkwardly on the grass, hugged and kissed the children before reaching over to kiss his mother on both cheeks.

"What are you doing here?" he asked her.

"You expect me to sit at home and wait for you to bring my grand-babies to me?" Doratea asked. "Saffron is lovely, such a brave girl. When are you going to marry her?"

Lucas rocked back on his heels to get up, but his mother held his wrist and pulled him down, patting the grass beside her.

Clumsily he sat on the soft grass, and the twins climbed onto his lap. He was used to his mother's directness, but at this precise moment he could do without it.

"I asked her once," Lucas said. "She said no."

"Ask her again."

"It's not that simple. I don't love her any more."

"You will have to re-learn then won't you, Gianluca. Where were you today?"

"At the other house."

"Doing what?"

"Working. Mama, why all the questions?"

"I ask because Saffron refused to discuss you, as though you had a fight. Have you been fighting, Gianluca?"

Doratea watched the guilty tinge of red flush his cheeks. She swatted him on the arm.

"You must treat the mother of your children with respect. Always!" she admonished. "You know how I feel about this. You have seen!" She drew in a deep breath. "Who is at this other house?"

Lucas cleared his throat. "I have a house guest staying."

"Male or female? No, let me answer. I know you will disappoint me and have a woman staying there. Stupido!" she said, swatting him on the arm again, harder this time.

125

"Stupido!" Nico shouted.

"Stupido," Bella said.

Doratea laughed. Lucas frowned.

"She's only a friend," Lucas said.

"And Saffron knows she is only a friend?"

"Saffron doesn't need to know what Rebecca is to me."

"Gianluca, you shame me," Doratea said with a shake of her head, causing several tendrils of silver hair to float out of the low chignon she wore. She looked at Lucas searchingly before shrugging with disapproval and then turning to the children with a song.

⁂

"Why didn't you tell me your mother was coming?" Saffron asked as soon as Lucas stepped into the house.

"I didn't know."

"I didn't know she was alive. You've never talked about her!" Saffron said.

"Protecting her is more of a habit, I guess," Lucas confessed. "My father tried to stop her from seeing me, but she wouldn't be stopped."

He put his hands in his pockets and smiled with tender remembrance. "We used to meet whenever she could slip away from the guards he had watching her. It wasn't often, but she managed it."

He smiled as he looked through the window, seeing his four-foot mother clap her small hands, teaching the children a popular Italian nursery rhyme. "You had better treat her kindly," Lucas said, suddenly turning from the window to pin Saffron in place with a glare.

Saffron put her hands on her hips. "When have I ever treated anyone badly?" she exclaimed, feeling offended.

"Cassidy?"

Saffron blanched and spun around to go into her bedroom.

Lucas followed her, closing the door behind him.

"Why don't you want to talk about her, Saffron?"

"It's none of your business."

"After me, she was the closest person to you. I don't understand why you won't talk about it."

Saffron walked to her wardrobe and pulled out a clean pair of jeans. "Will your mother be staying here?"

Lucas sighed and sat down on the edge of the bed to rub his head. Things were getting complicated. He'd planned to take the children back to England, have his lawyers purchase the property and not see Saffron ever again. But now, he was practically living with her. He'd been in Jamaica longer than he expected, and now his mother was here. Things couldn't get any worse.

"She can have my room," Lucas said.

Saffron stopped what she was doing and turned to look at Lucas. "And just where will you sleep?" she asked, eyeing him suspiciously.

"In here."

"I don't think so."

"Look, I'm not prepared to be anywhere other than with my children," Lucas said.

"You sleep on the couch. Take it or leave it." Saffron crossed her arms over her chest.

"What? Scared you can't control yourself if we share a bed, Saffron?" Lucas looked at her with a smile.

"Actually, yes," Saffron said.

He wasn't expecting such blatant honesty. He grabbed her arms and pulled her between his hard thighs.

"There is no reason why we can't sleep together," he teased, his eyes smouldering with sensuality. "We are consenting adults."

"No," Saffron said. "I value myself too much to sleep with you again."

"Being with me does not devalue you in any way!"

"Yes, it does. You don't respect me. You treat this place like a hotel, and I don't want you here complicating my life!"

"Are you pregnant?" Lucas asked, holding his breath. It had been bothering him all day, and he'd gone for a long drive along the coast to clear his head.

"No," Saffron replied.

"How do you know? It's too early to tell," Lucas announced as if he had expert knowledge of the cycle of her body. He tugged her down to sit on his lap.

"You've obviously thought about it," Saffron said.

"I'm prepared for every eventuality." Her breasts where level with his mouth.

"I'm on the pill."

He was not expecting to hear that. Why was she on the pill?

"If you have been entertaining other men in this house with my children in it, you are dead!"

Saffron gasped and tried to get up, but he held her down by wrapping his arms around her tiny waist.

"I'll pretend you didn't just say that," Saffron said.

"I'm warning you. No men!"

"Lucas, get over yourself. I'm a healthy woman with healthy needs and I–"

She got no further. Suddenly she was flat on her back on the bed, with Lucas leaning over her, looking into her brown eyes with fury. He pinned both of her arms above her head, holding her in place with one of his hands.

"I've said this before," Lucas snarled savagely, pressing his face menacingly close to hers. "No other men because I promise you, Saffron Noble, you will never see the twins again!"

"You don't mean that."

"Try me," Lucas said.

Their stared at each other for several seconds before Lucas released her and left the room.

"Well, I'll be off to bed now," Doratea announced not long after dinner. "It has been a long and emotional day for me." She kissed Saffron on both cheeks. "A day I will never forget!" she added, beaming at Saffron before turning to her son. "Gianluca, don't stay too long. Saffron needs to go to bed. The twins wake early."

Lucas looked at his mother. "I'm not going anywhere."

"Of course, you are. It is not proper that you stay here. Saffron is a single woman."

"If you are worried about Saffron's virtue, Mother, I can assure you she hasn't any!"

Saffron gasped as Doratea stood over Lucas, her frail hands on her tiny hips. She unleashed a barrage of hot Italian words that made Saffron wince. Saffron almost felt sorry for him, but she changed her mind. She cleared away the dinner plates, leaving him to his mother.

Saffron dumped the plates in the sink and soaped the sponge to wash and rinse the plates, using the smallest possible amount of water. She didn't get water through the pipes like the neighbours. She had her own water tank. Luckily it was positioned to catch the maximum amount of rainfall that slid off her roof and was almost always full.

Several minutes later, Lucas cleared his throat at the doorway. "I won't be staying here tonight," he announced.

Saffron turned to face him, the sponge still in her hand.

"I'll be over in the morning."

Saffron nodded.

"Say something," he prodded.

"I've nothing to say."

Lucas made a step towards her, his arms flung wide open. "Saffron, I–"

"Gianluca, say goodnight so that Saffron can go to bed!" Doratea ordered from the other room behind them, cutting him off.

"As tiny as she is, she has the disposition of a general," Lucas said, laughing.

"Good night, Saffron."

"Good night."

Chapter Eight

᷍᷍᷍᷍᷍᷍᷍

The beef patty and cherry box juice re-charged Saffron, and after a quick stretch, she threw away the empty food containers and pushed her way through the crowded fast food restaurant to get across the street.

She was in Ocho Rios and had been there all day, drumming up sponsorship and awareness for the church and its plight.

A week ago it had been decided that she was to preside over their fund raising intiative. So here she was, pavement pounding all day, dressed in a soft grey skirt, pale pink cotton blouse and a pair of three-inch heels that hadn't seen the light of day in over three years.

The street was filled with locals trying to get home for the evening. Nobody lined up. The mini buses pulled up anywhere and everywhere cramming in extra passengers.

Saffron arrived at the hairdresser's, glad she'd had the foresight to book an appointment in the morning. Almost two hours later, Saffron left the salon with fresh twists that now sported a funky auburn tint. She'd also had her eyebrows plucked and re-shaped. A young trainee had shyly asked if she could practise her make-up routine on her, so Saffron was now made up. She looked great and felt great.

Reaching home, she wound down her car window, reached out to the small metal box and punched in the four-digit security code. The gate wasn't the huge eyesore she had feared it would be, and even the chain-link fence Lucas had insisted on erecting wasn't a problem. It was too far away to be seen. Mas Arthur loved using the gate.

Doratea had the twins and wasn't home yet. Saffron unlocked the front door. She was about to enter the house when a car horn blasted several times from the gate.

Roderick leaned out the window and waved. Saffron waved back, went into the house and pressed the internal button to open the gate and waited for Roderick on the verandah.

"What wid di high tech gate?" Roderick asked after he kissed Saffron on each cheek and sat down.

"Lucas had it installed," Saffron replied.

"So him still deh bout," Roderick said with a raised eyebrow.

Saffron was relieved to hear his natural Jamaican accent instead of the overly dramatised British accent he was using a few weeks ago.

"Yes, he's still here," Saffron answered and went on to tell Roderick about his mistake with the legal papers.

Roderick was horrified, and after finishing off the juice Saffron had brought him, he stood to say goodbye. He hugged her tightly and then pressed something into her hand.

"What's this?" Saffron asked, looking at the folded paper.

"That's fi every ting, Saffy," he said, holding her hands. "Mi was not a good person to you, and mi did tek advantage."

Saffron opened the folded paper to see a cheque with a mind-boggling figure written on it.

"I can't accept this," she said, trying to hand it back to him, but Roderick stepped back and held up his palms.

"Saffy, mi heart bleeding ova di way mi used to be. Please tek it, if not for you den fi di pickney dem."

Saffron shook her head and pushed the cheque into Roderick breast pocket before turning to walk down the shallow steps to his car.

With her back to him, Roderick quickly slipped inside the house and wedged the cheque beneath the fruit bowl.

Lucas turned off the local radio station that had been playing dance-hall music as he turned into the drive. He stopped in front of the gate, punched in the code and counted the ten seconds it took for the gate to open wide enough for him to drive through.

He noticed the strange car before he saw Saffron and Roderick kissing beside it. A rage like none he had ever felt before exploded inside him, completely ereasing his good mood.

With Roderick's arms still around her shoulders, Saffron turned at the sound of the approaching car which came to a slow stop beside them.

She ignored the pang of excitement that always coursed within her whenever Lucas was near. She noticed an ominous expression on his face as he slammed the car door and walked towards them.

With a gentleness that belied the savage fury in his smouldering stare, Lucas pulled Saffron from Roderick's arms and swung a powerful fist, hitting Roderick squarely in the face.

Saffron gasped in shock as Roderick fell against the car and slid down to the ground, holding his jaw.

Lucas hauled him up by the shirt and hit him again.

"No!" Saffron shouted, grabbing Lucas's arm just as he was about to hit Roderick again. "What are you doing? You bloody savage!"

Lucas said nothing, turned on his heel and strolled to the house with his hands in his pockets.

"Are you all right?" Saffron asked Roderick as he stumbled to his feet, shaking his head as though to clear it.

"Don't you touch me!" Roderick shouted, stepping away as if Saffron was a live electrical wire. "Mi like mi face de way it is, tanks," he continued before adding, "Bwoy, Saffy, di boy have some strong feelings a gwaan fi you."

"Don't be ridiculous," Saffron said. "Lucas only wants me in his bed, nothing else."

"You tink so? Any man a go hit another man with bloodclaat murder in his eyes mus love you bad bad."

Saffron turned to the house, seeing Lucas watching them from the window.

"Mi better go before him come finish mi off," Roderick said, getting into his car. "You'll be ok?"

"I'll be fine," Saffron replied, rubbing the back of her neck. "Good-bye, Roderick."

"See ya, Saffy. I'll sort out di mix-up wid di papers dem and ring you from Ingland," Roderick said as he stuck two fingers up in Lucas's direction. Then, reversing, he tooted his car horn loudly before driving away.

Saffron watched him go through the gate then turned to the house. Lucas was still watching her. She could feel his harsh stare burn through her. With a toss of her head, she walked up to the house. As soon as the screen door slammed behind her, Lucas approached her.

"Where are the children?" he asked through his tightly clenched teeth. His hands were balled into tight fists at his side.

"With your mother, but—,"

"I thought I told you I didn't want that degenerate anywhere near you?"

"For God's sake, calm down. You don't own me, and I don't appreciate you going around hitting my friends," Saffron said.

Lucas stomped towards her and grabbed her arm. "I come home and you're wearing a skirt, heels and make-up for another man, and you think I should be calm!" he bellowed.

"I've been out!"

"Out where?"

"The day I have to report my whereabouts to you I will be six feet under!" Saffron said trying hard to pull out of his grasp.

"You don't leave this house unless me or Muzio is with you," Lucas ordered.

Saffron laughed. Lucas's eyes darkened and his fingers dug into her arm.

"You're hurting me," Saffron winced.

Lucas looked down at his fingers and then let her go.

"What did he want?" he asked, trying to calm down.

"I don't want to fight with you."

"If you don't want to fight then you'd better answer my question."

Saffron put her hands to her hips. "Taking that attitude with me will get you nowhere. In fact, there's the door, use it!"

"I demand an answer," Lucas insisted.

"Go to hell!"

They stood staring at each other, the tension increasing by the second. It was Lucas who turned away first.

"I was in Ocho Rios on business and getting my hair done," Saffron said.

"Was that so hard?"

"Actually it was," Saffron said. "The only person I answer to is myself. So save yourself another jealous rage from here on out because I do what I please."

Lucas bristled, a tide of colour flushing his cheeks. "I am not jealous," he said, shoving his balled fists into his pockets.

Saffron looked at him. "Whatever. I'm going to shower."

Scowling, Lucas scooped up an otaheite apple from the fruit basket to stop himself from following her. Yet again she had managed to have the last word. What had she been doing in Ocho Rios anyway? What business did she go on? Lucas asked himself, as a piece of paper fluttered to the ground.

He picked it up and unfolded it as he bit into the fruit.

"Saffron!"

"Yes?" she answered, walking back into the living room, her shoulders drooping.

"What's this?"

"This what?"

Lucas held out the paper to her and Saffron realized that it was the cheque Roderick had tried to give her.

"Is this for services rendered?" Lucas asked, catching the hand that Saffron was about to hit him with. He shook his head and released her hand before moving away.

"I tried to give it back to him, but he must have slipped it somewhere. Where was it?"

"Don't give me that. You won't take anything from me, but you take from him."

"It's not like that!"

Lucas sliced the air with his hands viciously. "This is it."

"What do you mean?" Saffron asked.

Suddenly Lucas grabbed her shoulders and kissed her ferociously.

Saffron struggled but her strength was nothing when compared to Lucas's raging force. With ease he walked her backwards until her back hit the cool wall. He lifted her, tipping her off balance so that she had to grab his broad shoulders for balance.

Her smooth, honey-coloured legs wrapped around his hips as he quickly lifted up her skirt, and then, with a loud grunt, skimmed a lean hand along her panties and pushed the silky lace aside.

Within seconds, he was inside her and pumping away as though his life depended on it.

The sex was fast and satisfying, and when it was over, it left both of them even more confused than before.

"That's it. The games stop here," Lucas said eventually, still breathing hard. "I didn't use anything," he added, turning away to fix his trousers. Before Saffron could say anything Lucas left the room. A minute later, she heard him drive off.

The following day, Doratea greeted Saffron with some big news: There was another aggressive takeover bid, and the bank was under threat. Lucas would have to leave the island for several days, which could actually turn into weeks.

Saffron poured herself a glass of water and sat on a stool to drink it. Saffron hoped Doratea had heard about the hurricane alert, and with a worried frown, she stood to rinse the glass.

That's when she saw it. Nico's toy elephant. It was on the floor by a lounger outside. Doratea couldn't have left it as Nico could be a little terror without it. Going outside and picking it up, Saffron dialled Doratea's number again and again. It went to voice mail. She cursed herself for not having a number for Muzio. Saffron's concern quickly became a glacier of momentous panic. Something was wrong.

Dashing inside, she burst into Lucas's office and cried with frustration when she realized he wasn't there. Scrambling around, she opened every door in the house and called his name, not caring if he was having sex with his little playmate Rebecca.

"Saffron, I didn't hear you all come back?" Lucas said, wrapping a towel around his waist. He was tired, having been travelling from London to Italy and New York, trying to make sense of the takeover bid. Fortunately, the aggressive company had suddenly withdrawn.

"Have you seen your mother?" Saffron asked, trying not to panic.

"No, why? I thought she was out with you?"

"No, I've been at work," Saffron replied.

"Work?"

"Yes. Doratea keeps the children while I'm working. But she's not here!" Saffron cried. "She's always here!"

Lucas was still stuck on what she had just said about working and had to shake his head to focus on the other things she was saying. "I'm sure she's fine. Muzio is with her."

"Look." Saffron shoved Nico's toy in his face. "Your mother knows not to leave it, and I can't get her on her mobile!"

"Calm down."

"Don't tell me to calm down! Something is wrong. I know it."

Lucas spun away and went to the walk-in wardrobe, where he flung off the towel, pulled on white cotton boxers, dark olive chinos and a black t-shirt.

"Ring Muzio," he ordered.

"I don't have his number. He doesn't speak to me."

Lucas rang his mother's number then tried Muzio, but he got no answer.

Saffron was now making a meal of her bottom lip and looking absolutely petrified. Lucas walked to the pool house with her hot on his heels.

"Rebecca," Lucas called out. Rebecca strolled out of the bedroom in a tiny white bikini, fanning her freshly painted nails. "Have you seen my mother?"

"Not since this morning," Rebecca answered in a bored tone without looking up.

"And!" Lucas prompted sharply.

"And," Rebecca sighed melodramatically, "a black van came and picked her up and that hulk of a bodyguard followed right after in his Jeep thing," she added, staring at her nails.

"What time was this?"

"I have no idea. Time stays still on the island."

"Becca," Lucas said, walking forward and placing his hands on her naked shoulders. "I need you to tell me everything you saw, ok?"

"Okay," she replied, eager to please. Lucas had brought her a lovely diamond bracelet ealier. "There was this old guy, who looked a bit like you actually," she said. "Yeah, he was old and had silver hair. Your mother looked a bit green and was arguing with him. Then he sort of grabbed her and the brats," Rebecca added, shrugging.

"What else," Lucas urged, looking pale beneath his tan. "What else!" He shook Rebecca.

"Gianluca, you're hurting me!" Rebecca cried.

"I'm sorry." He let her go and forced himself to soften his tone. "What else."

"Muzio came dashing around the house and followed them."

Lucas cursed long and hard and spun around, almost tripping over Saffron as he dialled a number into his phone and starting speaking urgently in Italian. As he spoke, he caught Saffron's elbow and led her back to the main house.

A few minutes later Lucas looked at her, his eyes bleak and as cold as the North Sea. Saffron shivered and wrapped her arms around herself.

"What is it?" she asked.

Lucas breathed in deeply. "Muzio's Jeep has been found abandoned in a gully."

"But what about the twins? Your mother?"

"My security team is on it. They'll ring me as soon as they find something out."

"No! I need to know what's going on now. Who's taken the twins?" Saffron cried out. It was only when Lucas pushed her into a chair that she realised just how badly she was shaking.

Lucas's phone rang and he turned his back on her. Saffron strained to hear any word she might recognise, but he was talking too fast.

When he finished the call, he didn't turn to her immediately, but she could sense his tension.

"Please, Lucas, what is it?" She walked up to him and touched his arm.

"He isn't dead."

"Who isn't dead?" Saffron asked.

"My father. He isn't dead."

"But I thought...?"

"Exactly. We all thought. Bastardo! He has the children and Mama."

"Oh, my God!" Saffron cried. "But why? I don't understand."

Lucas looked at Saffron's distraught face. "I'm sorry."

"I don't want you to be bloody sorry. I want you to get my children back!" she screamed at him. Lucas was behaving like a frightened little boy about to get a beating.

"He can't hurt you any more, Lucas," Saffron said, shaking him. "Now get yourself together and go get our family back!"

The first gust of wind blew in the early evening and soon developed into a strong gale. The hurricane was due to hit the island by nightfall. The rain hadn't yet started, but it was coming. Dark clouds in a pattern Saffron had never seen before blanketed the sky, almost obliterating the late evening sun.

Lucas had learned of his mother's suspicions through one of the security personnel. She thought she had glimpsed her husband at a fête and had beefed up her security, and moved Saffron and the children to Lucas's place, knowing it would be more secure without arousing Saffron's suspicions. But why hadn't she told him? Lucas asked himself.

His phone rang, interrupting his stream of thoughts.

His father had been spotted at the Norman Manley Airport in Kingston, trying to leave the country. But all planes were now grounded due to the weather. Thanking God, Lucas grabbed his car keys and headed outside.

"Where are you going?" Saffron asked, hugging Nico's elephant to her breast.

"He's been spotted at the airport."

"Are the children with him?"

"I'm going to find out now."

"I'm going with you."

"No. You stay here," Lucas ordered.

"No!"

"Saffron, it's not safe. I need you to stay. Please."

Biting her lips, Saffron nodded.

Lucas leaned down and kissed her forehead. "Good girl. I'll be back as soon as I can with the twins and my mama."

"I know you will," Saffron said with an encouraging smile. "Promise me you'll be careful?"

"I promise," he replied, kissing her lips.

The rain started and the heavy wind intensified by the minute. Needing something to do, Saffron secured all the outdoor garden furniture in the shed. Catching sight of Rebecca lounging in the pool house, she went and invited her to come up to the main house. Rebecca refused.

With a shrug, Saffron closed all the windows, took out the candles and matches and placed kerosene-filled hurricane lamps strategically around the house. It was only a matter of time before the power went. When everything was in order, Saffron used the remote to lower the hurricane shutters on the windows and doors.

She then made herself a sandwich and forced it down while listening to the radio announcer forecast doom as Hurricane Maddox drew closer to the island.

The house rumbled and the overhead lights flickered once and then twice. The wind howled bitterly, making Saffron shudder with fright. She could hear the rain on the tiled roof, battering away in rhythmic waves as the wind picked up. Her poor babies must be scared out of their minds, she thought. But thank God, Doratea was with them.

The house trembled and the lights flickered until there was nothing but darkness. Saffron lit a candle and sat in a chair with her legs curled beneath her. She was scared and lonely and would do anything to have her babies with her. She began to sob.

A loud crash at the side of the house, followed by a freezing cold gust of wind sweeping through the living room, made Saffron scream. Rubbing the tears from her cheek with hands that shook, she went to the kitchen and stood by the door. Rain splashed inside and onto the marble floor. She could see a branch sticking through the ceiling. Realizing there was nothing she could do, Saffron closed the door.

If Lucas's house was getting such a battering, she couldn't even begin to imagine how hers and Mas Arthur's were faring.

Suddenly worried about Mas Arthur, Saffron quickly climbed through a small porthole in the helper's quarters and made her way outside.

She was drenched within seconds. The rain was coming down in heavy grey sheets. She could barely see, but she ploughed on, wrestling with the wind to get her car door open. She was relieved when she was finally inside the vehicle and was able to drive out onto the main road.

The scenery was horrible. She drove slowly, thanking her angels that she knew every curve and bump of the road. She couldn't see anything past the beam of her headlights. The windscreen wipers worked in frantic overtime, trying in vain to swish away the water. She turned on the radio for company, but there was only a static hiss where all the channels used to be, so she turned it off.

Saffron drove on, her small car sometimes lifting off the road as the gale force winds blew. She was frightened, but she had to get to Mas Arthur. She skidded on mud that had slipped down the mountainside onto the road, and drove around uprooted trees and debris. No other vehicles were on the road. Her head ached from the intense concentration, and her eyes watered as she strained to see where she was going.

Through her headlights she saw the outline of a huge tree leaning dangerously into the road. It's many branches scraped across the bonnet and side of her car with a terrifying screech. Saffron screamed and bent down, protecting her head with her arms as the branches thumped her windscreen.

Saffron peeped over the steering wheel and slammed her fist against it with frustration as she realized that the tree had fallen across the road, blocking her path. There was no way around it.

She stared at it, frozen for a long time and unable to process anything in her mind. She didn't know what to do, but then a decision was made for her as the car nudged to the left on its own. Frowning, Saffron reached over to the passenger window to wind it down.

A stream of muddy water rushed towards her. The tree had created a dam, and the water forged a new path directly in line with Saffron's car. Panicking in the darkness, Saffron pushed against the door, trying to open it but couldn't as the current was too powerful.

She moved back to the driver's side just as the car began to bob precariously. Water seeped through every crevice. Panicking, she opened her door and stepped out.

The water reached her shins and was rapidly rising. It was freezing cold. The raging water splashed against her tense calves.

Reaching for the tree branches, Saffron hauled herself up onto the bonnet and slid down in front of the car. The water was rising rapidly, and fearing she may be swept away, she quickly pulled herself from branch to branch until she reached the tree trunk.

She hugged the rough bark and caught her breath. The car had shifted sideways, its lights now facing the mountainside.

Climbing over the tree trunk, Saffron fought her way out of the tangled tree limbs and began to walk. She could barely see but trudged on through the water, thinking past the pain in her legs.

It was a relief to recognise her driveway, and Saffron hurriedly tried to climb the gate, but it was too wet and slippery. Frantically she kicked off her shoes and climbed onto the chain-link fence beside the gate post and jumped down to the other side to run to Mas Arthur's.

The place was in utter darkness. She banged on his front door before going around his little house for any sign of life. He wasn't there. Saffron felt like crying.

The adrenalin that had got her to this point disappeared abruptly. She had nothing left, and in tears she went to her own house. The windows had been destroyed, and the railings on the verandah were dancing madly in tune with the wind.

Realising she'd lost her keys somewhere along the way, Saffron laughed silently. Why use the door when she could climb through a window? There were pieces of jagged glass sticking out of the splintered window frame, and she carefully climbed over them.

The rain was coming down heavily through the roof, and the banging sound of clashing metal above her head was frightening. The roof was about to go at any minute.

She couldn't stay here, she thought hurrying through the window, again not realising that she had cut herself until she felt the hot flow of blood as it gushed from a deep gash at her wrist. The old house groaned as if in pain.

Fighting through her own pain, Saffron crawled along the verandah and down the steps but fell as something hit her on the left temple, and for a moment all Saffron saw was bright white light.

She needed shelter and fast, she thought, feeling light-headed. She felt entranced all of a sudden, as she looked at blood oozing from her cut.

She fell again, hitting her knees hard on the rain-soaked ground. She couldn't think and didn't know where she was, but felt a sodden line of rope with her hands. She grabbed at it, following it like a lifeline. Saffron laughed and cried, her tears mixing with the rain.

Suddenly, she wasn't getting wet any more. She tried to understand, but thinking made her head hurt. Her knees hurt and her cut hurt. She didn't want to hurt any more. Feeling the warmth of a furry blanket close by she lay down and curled into the darkness.

⁂

Nobody had seen or heard from Saffron since the night before. She'd taken her car, and again Lucas cursed himself for not getting rid of the damn thing. The only place she could have gone was to her own house.

He hadn't slept in nearly four days and was beginning to feel the weight of exhaustion. But at least the problem of his father was gone. For now anyway. It had been the old man behind all the aggressive takeover bids at the bank, just to keep Lucas on his toes, he'd said, making sure the Conti-Bridgewater empire stayed at the top. There was no explanation about the supposed death, and Lucas didn't ask.

Lucas told him in a few choice words that messing with his family was the last straw and demanded that he quit. Lucas booked his mother and the twins into a hotel in New Kingston. Muzio was with them and he'd ordered extra security.

Once the weather had improved, his father had greased the palm of a pilot, commandeered a small private plane, and against all precautions had left the island.

Heading to Saffron's house, Lucas had to stop several times to move a tree and other debris from the road, making the usually half-hour long journey nearly three times as long.

When he saw Saffron's little red car wedged against a tree, he felt as terrified as he did when the children had gone missing.

The car was covered in mud and was empty. Lucas drove on, stopping when he saw Miss Hyacinth sweeping water from her house. Mas Arthur was with her, and after making sure they were okay, he went to the house.

He parked at the gate and got out looking about in dismay. All that was left of the house was the stone fireplace and three partial walls. The outside wall to the children's room was gone. Everything was scattered about, wet and ruined. Large sheets of aluminium that must have been the roof lay twisted and bent like play dough.

Climbing with ease over the gate, he dropped down on the other side and jogged to the house. He called out Saffron's name, but the only answer he got was the pathetic bleating from the goats, which had been tied to the verandah post.

He walked around the house, his mouth flattening into a grim white line. As much as he'd wanted to hate this place, he had loved it's quirkiness. Now everything was soaking wet and dripping.

"Saffron!" he called out again. Mas Arthur had been safe staying with Miss Hyacinth, so she wouldn't have gone up there. Walking through what was once the front door, Lucas looked around for a clue but found nothing.

Descending the steps, he tripped over the rope securing the goats. He untied it to move them to the bushes so they could feed until Mas Arthur came and sorted them out.

Pulling hard, he tried to coax them out from under the house and dropped down to his knees to see why they wouldn't budge.

That was when he saw the blood. Large blobs of blood stained the grass, and he followed the trail until he was on his stomach and crawling under the house.

Surrounded by a small herd of goats, Saffron lay fast asleep.

"Come on, Saff," Lucas urged, crawling over to her. She wasn't moving and was lying at an odd angle. Her clothes were dirty and torn and stuck to her body.

Quickly, he pushed the numerous goats aside. As soon as he moved it, she moaned but didn't open her eyes. She'd been unconscious. Running his hands urgently over her body, he found numerous cuts and scrapes but nothing that could warrant the amount of blood he had seen.

Frowning, he pulled her gently from under the house and checked her over again. There was a large bump on her temple and a huge bruise on one side of her face. He used his mobile phone to call for help.

The goats followed him out and watched him keenly. One goat was covered in blood on one side. Lucas looked for a cut on the animal and then checked Saffron again. A steady stream of blood had begun to trickle from her wrist to the grass.

Tearing his shirt tail, he tied the cloth tightly on her upper arm, and almost immediately the blood flow slowed. Scooping her up, he frantically ran to the gate, yelling for help.

Chapter Nine

$\mathcal{T}$he steady beep beep of the hospital machinery almost lulled Lucas into a dreamy sleep. But he was too exhausted to sleep; the hard orange plastic chair on which he sat was apparently not made for comfort. The strong smell of disinfectant was equally unbearable.

He held Saffron's slender hand. It was warm and was being supported by the several wires and tubes connected to her.

Every time Lucas closed his eyes, he saw Saffron lying on the back seat of the Jeep, pale and not breathing as he rushed her to the hospital.

That was two days ago, and still Saffron lay unconscious. The doctors didn't know what had caused her comatose state, whether it was the cut on her wrist directly on a major artery, or the huge bump on her head. The bruise surrounding the bump was massive, all blacks, purples and blues, marring her brown skin down one side of her face.

The door opened.

"Have you been home yet, sa?" the short, pigeon-chested doctor on duty asked, walking to the end of the bed and picking up Saffron's chart. "Any changes?"

"None," Lucas replied.

"Hmm. Yes, well," the doctor mumbled, checking the reading on the medical paraphernalia before staring at Lucas over the rim of his narrow wired glasses. "You won't be much good for Miss Saffron if you don't go home and get some rest."

Lucas didn't know whether to be touched or annoyed at the doctor's utterance. "I'm fine," he answered dismissively, rubbing his thumb pad over Saffron's knuckles.

"Yes, well, my wife and Miss Saffron are good friends, you know."

"Yes, I do know. You told me that the last time you were here."

"She sent some soup. One of the nurses is hotting it up for you."

Lucas gave the old doctor his full attention.

"Your wife did that for me?" he asked bewildered. He didn't know the man's wife. "But she doesn't even know me."

"Well, you are Miss Saffron's baby daddy, and we all look after our own. So I'll send the nurse in wid it soon."

Lucas was touched.

"Tell your wife many thanks for me, Doctor. It is greatly appreciated."

The doctor smiled and left the room.

Nurse Green, whom he had met briefly the last time he was at the hospital, brought in a huge glass bowl of reddish-brown soup. She moved the bed tray from the foot of Saffron's bed and positioned it for Lucas to use.

"There you go," Nurse Green said.

"Thank you, Nurse Green."

"No need to thank me, Mr Lucas. Miss Saffron would never forgive us if we let you starve."

Lucas chuckled. The sudden movement of his lips felt unfamiliar.

"It's red peas soup, with what looks like every ting in it," Nurse Green was saying.

After she left the room Lucas moved the table aside and went to the window. His eyes were hazy with tears.

He looked out at the many beheaded palm trees in the distance and the debris from the hurricane still scattered across the hospital grounds.

The soup tasted very good, and Lucas was just finishing off a skinny dumpling when the door opened. It was the doctor again.

"Please thank your wife for the lovely meal," Lucas said.

The doctor beamed and nodded, but then frowned down at the notes he was reading.

With a sigh he turned to Lucas. "We'll have to move her," he said.

"Move her?" Lucas asked perplexed. "To where?"

"Kingston. We just don't have the equipment here to treat her properly, and to be honest, I don't understand why she isn't conscious yet. We need to do some tests, but we don't have the equipment here."

"I see." Lucas couldn't think straight.

"I'll arrange it. If you can help Nurse Green bring in another bed you can sleep on that tonight."

"But I thought we're going to Kingston."

"Too late for tonight. We'll keep Miss Saffron stable, and tomorrow you will hire a helicopter as a lot of roads are still blocked, and take her to University Hospital. They are expecting her first thing in the morning."

"Okay," Lucas replied.

The doctor left, and after helping Nurse Green with the bed, Lucas pushed it as close to Saffron as he could get, called his mother and then went to sleep holding Saffron's hand.

❧❦❧❦

There wasn't any particular medical reason why Saffron hadn't regained consciousness. All medical tests done at the University Hospital said so.

So everyone waited, talked to her, brought her favourite music in, but still she didn't wake.

The doctors assumed it was because of an event she didn't want to face, and Lucas, knowing that the children had been taken hours before

Hurricane Maddox had hit, believed that was the reason. He'd thought about bringing the children in but banished the thought almost immediately. Seeing their mother like this was bound to upset them.

So he sat, read to Saffron and talked to her until the days turned into weeks. Still no response.

❧•❦ ❧•❦

Saffron could hear what was going on around her, but she couldn't open her eyes or respond in any way. It was as though she was hearing everything through a frosted pane of glass; able to tell night from day, but unable to see anything.

Lucas was with her. He was reading the paper, a large paper. She could tell. The rustling was loud each time he turned a page. He was reading her horoscope aloud.

The paper rustled again and a chair scraped. She knew she was in the hospital as Lucas had told her, but she didn't know why she was here. Another pair of footsteps, and then Lucas touched her hand, raising it to his lips. She could feel the warmth of his breath as he kissed her palm.

"I'm going to get a coffee and then I'll be back," he told her, turning her hand to kiss her knuckles before gently laying her hand onto the cool bed sheet.

Someone else was in the room now. Every time Lucas left the room someone else came in. It was a woman. Saffron could smell her perfume.

"Your husband sent me in again," the woman said. "Bwoy, him very forceful, but him nice. Him never lef yuh side since yuh been under."

Husband? Saffron asked herself. She and Lucas were married?

"Him have all di nurses dem sweet," the woman said, chuckling.

The door opened again. Coffee. Saffron could smell strong black coffee.

"Thank you, Nurse," Lucas said.

149

"'Tis a pleasure, sir."

Saffron could almost hear the flirtatious smile in the nurse's voice.

Lucas began talking again, and Saffron listened, wanting to reply. When Lucas told her he loved her and squeezed her hand, she wanted to respond, but the words stuck frozen and silent in her throat.

❧⠀☙⠀❧⠀☙

September turned to October. Lucas's mother wanted to move out of the hotel and back into the house now that the roof and kitchen had been repaired. One of the trees on the property fell on it during the passage of the hurricane.

Lucas had bought the land Saffron had been fighting him for and donated it back to the church on the condition that there would be no re-sale.

Saffron was moved back to Port Antonio Hospital, and Lucas thought about employing a nurse and taking Saffron home.

The only time he left her side was on a Sunday when his mother came to take over so he could stay with the children. He was warned that Saffron's coma could go on for years, and he prepared himself for that possibility.

October turned to November. Saffron continually recieved a steady stream of visitors, from congregation members from her church to the hairdresser in Ocho Rios who'd asked Lucas if she could do Saffron's hair. Lucas was touched by all the love and support they showed, which was also extended to him and his mother.

On one particular afternoon, when Saffron had visitors from church, they prayed and then left the room, and Saffron thought she was alone again. But two people were whispering closely. She couldn't quite catch what they were saying, but she heard the names Nico and Bella. Something tugged at her mind but then slipped away, leaving her puzzled and confused.

Who were Nico and Bella? Were they important? Why hadn't Lucas told her about them?

Lucas came back in. He tucked her hand into his and she tried to squeeze.

"I'm thinking of opening a pub, Saff," he told her and began to outline his plans. It would be a typical English pub and sports bar. Jamaicans loved their sports, Lucas said with growing enthusiasm.

She remembered the coffee bar in Nottingham and the pleasure it gave Lucas. Did he live in Jamaica now?

"It's Sunday tomorrow, Saff, and I'll be gone for the day. Mama will be here with you, ok, my love?" he explained, touching her cheek. She tried to move into it.

"Saff, you moved!" Lucas cried, pressing the emergency button to the nurses' station.

A nurse rushed in.

"She moved," Lucas explained excitedly. "I was telling her about tomorrow, and I touched her face and she moved her head."

"You sure you never move 'gainst di pillow an her head move?" the nurse asked.

"I'm sure." Lucas placed his hand against Saffron's cheek. "Move again for me, Saff?" he asked gently and waited. Nothing.

There, Lucas, I'm moving for you, Saffron wanted to say.

Lucas watched her carefully, waiting for movement, any movement, but withdrew his hand after several long minutes. Nothing.

The nurse looked at him, her eyes full of sympathy, before going around the bed to touch his arm gently. "Sometimes when we want something bad bad, it might look like it fi real," she explained, softly squeezing Lucas's arm before leaving.

Lucas frowned, looking at Saffron. He knew she had moved. He didn't imagine it.

It was time for something drastic, Lucas thought days later. Saffron obviously was not going to come back to them on her own; she needed something to motivate her. Saffron was a fighter. She just needed some cause to fight for.

She'd been living her life in limbo. Jamaica was her refuge. She'd run away from England and practically hid herself away in a tiny community between two major towns, and that's where she was in life now. In the in-between.

At university, Saffron was on the honour roll, she was on the debate team and played competitive sports. After university it was a race between them to see who could set up their business first. Saffron needed a goal. She needed to come out of this coma that had really started three years ago. It was time for Plan B.

Chapter Ten

"*I*ve brought you home, Saff," Lucas explained to Saffron, once Nurse Green had settled her in and they were alone.

Home? Saffron asked herself.

"It's not your house, because that's, well, in need of some work," Lucas said awkwardly. "This is the house where I've been staying and you were here for a time."

I remember, Saffron said to herself.

"Nurse Green will be living here and looking after you. Every morning you'll be having some physio and exercise," Lucas explained. "As you know I don't like my women too curvy."

He did not just say that!

"Then I'll be taking you into the pool for some more exercises. The doctors said it'd be okay as long as you don't overdo it. But I can tell you now, I'm going to work you hard."

Are you really? If she could move, Saffron would have thumped him one already.

You've spent too much time lazing around!

The bloody nerve. Go to hell!

"I know you can hear me, Saff, as I can practically feel you screaming at me." Lucas smiled, he was enjoying himself.

Stuff it.

"I'll let you settle as I've got some calls to make. See you later. Don't go anywhere." He finished with a chuckle, closing the door behind him.

Don't go anywhere?! Saffron fumed silently trying to wiggle her toes. She felt frustrated. All of the doctors had said there was no particular medical reason to explain why she wasn't moving, as she had responded to touch. They said she was mentally blocking signals to her brain and they had no idea why.

❧❦❧❦

"Gianluca," Doratea said as she entered her son's office without knocking, catching him staring into space with his feet on the desk. His face was grim and his eyes shadowed with sadness. He looked up and plastered on a smile, but Doratea wasn't fooled.

"Hi, Mama," Lucas stood and walked over to his tiny mother, taking her hands and kissing her on both cheeks. "What's up?"

"I am concerned, Gianluca," Doratea sighed as she relaxed into a chair. "You aren't eating and you aren't talking. I don't like seeing you like this."

Lucas rubbed his forehead tiredly. "I'm fine."

"No! You are not fine." And then with a swift change of subject that was typical she went on to ask, "Have you heard anything from your father?"

"He's in Europe somewhere, no doubt scrambling about trying to hold everything together with the whip and chains he likes to employ," Lucas said. "He's too busy to bother about us for the moment."

"That's what I don't like Gianluca; not knowing what he is going to do next. We need to keep the children safe."

"As long as you stay in Jamaica you will be safe. I will make sure that nothing happens to any of you."

Doratea smiled and walked around the desk to him. "You are a good boy, Gianluca, but you shoulder too much. Tell Saffron about the children. There is nothing like a mother's love."

They had talked about this before just a few weeks ago. Maybe his mother was right Lucas thought. The children may just give Saffron the jolt she needs to come back to them. He'd tried everything else.

He ran his hands through his over long hair. "Soon, Mother," he promised. "Soon."

⊱⋅⋄⋅⊰

The door opened and Saffron strained to hear the sounds of footsteps but only heard a soft pat-pat she didn't recognise.

She could smell something sweet, maybe honey or maybe guava jam, she didn't know which. Her bed sheet moved and a tiny hand touched her arm.

"Mummy?" a small voice said.

Mummy? Who was this child? And why was it calling her Mummy?

The sheets moved again and the bed dipped as the child climbed onto the bed and sat close to Saffron.

"Mummy?"

It was a little girl. Where had she come from?

"Mummy sleeping?" the little girl asked. "Bella sleeping too."

Bella? I've heard that name before.

The little girl snuggled into Saffron's neck and stayed there.

⊱⋅⋄⋅⊰

"Gianluca, we have a little problem," Doratea said a short time after their talk in his office.

Lucas raised his dark eyebrows.

"Come," his mother ordered and walked ahead of him. He followed her into Saffron's room, and there was Bella with her three fingers in her mouth, fast asleep snuggled into her mother's side.

Lucas felt a pain rip through his heart, seeing the two of them together like that. His mother moved to the side of the bed and put a

155

pillow behind Bella's back, so she wouldn't roll off, and then with a soft smile took her son's arm and led him away.

"When Bella wakes, you will tell Saffron about the children," she told him softly.

"Yes," Lucas said, feeling a lump in his throat.

He wanted his family back. He wanted Saffron to wear his ring and carry his last name. He wanted them to be a family living normally and having more children. He could feel the heavy weight of his problems bearing down on him. He didn't know what to do and couldn't do anything until Saffron woke up. And then, who knew what state her mind would be in? What if she didn't remember any of them? What if she remembered that she loved someone else?

Later that night, Lucas went into Saffron's room and sat on the side of the bed looking down at her. She'd lost a lot of weight and it worried him. Her cheekbones were more prominent and her arms and fingers looked ridiculously fragile.

"Saff," he said, taking her hand and rubbing his thumb over the long thin scar inside her narrow wrist.

He started the story at the beginning, from their time as best friends in Nottingham, her shop, their friends and then finally what had brought her to Jamaica. He told her about the twins and searched for some response from her as he repeated what she had told him about the difficult pregnancy, their birth and the nappy rash incident.

He told her about his father and the hurricane, leaving nothing out. He was also building her a new home to replace the one destroyed by Hurrican Maddox. He apologised for not telling her sooner, and when he finished hours later, he kissed her goodnight and left the room.

It was all too much for Saffron to take in at one time. She had twins — a boy and a girl! Bella and Nico. She was upset that she hadn't remembered them. What kind of mother forgot her own children? She couldn't picture their faces. Who did they look like? How old were they? She'd wanted to ask Lucas to describe them, but the words didn't pass her throat.

She remembered the hurricane, she remembered the furry blankets, but she didn't remember her own children.

Saffron cried, tears seeped from beneath her closed lids, disappearing into her hair.

❧ ⋈ ❧

"Gianluca, you need to go to Ocho Rios to look for a location," Doratea said one afternoon when she caught her son walking around the house aimlessly with his hands in his pockets. The twins were napping after visiting their mother. Lucas had put Saffron through vigorous training that morning.

"For what?" Lucas asked his mother.

"For the pub you are starting, naturally."

He smiled, but shook his head. His dark hair flopped into his eyes. "I have to stay here."

"No, Muzio is here. We are safe. Go and have a nice long drive. If we need you I will ring. Now go!" she ordered, pushing him out the front door. She beamed brightly as she waved him off. The change of scenery would do him good.

❧ ⋈ ❧

Bella was with Saffron again. The little girl would come into her room and talk to her before climbing off the bed and disappearing again.

157

"Mummy?" Bella asked. "Mummy sleeping again?"

No, my darling, I can hear you.

"Mummy, you sing to Bella?"

I can't baby.

"Mummy, you sing to Bella now!" the little girl screamed with tears in her eyes, not understanding why Mummy wouldn't play along.

Bella climbed onto the bed and sat on Saffron's stomach. "Mummy no like Bella no more?" she asked with a tremble in her voice.

I love you sweetheart, I do! Oh God, please someone take her away.

"Bella sing, then Mummy love Bella. Yes?"

> *Clap your tiny hands*
> *Clap your tiny hands*
> *Clap your tiny hands*
> *for joy.*

Bella clapped just above Saffron's nose, and as if watching a large television screen, Saffron saw herself singing the same song to the children sitting on the grass in front of a wooden house! She was starting to remember.

> *Jesus loves to hear*
> *little children sing*
> *Clap your tiny hands*
> *for joy.*
> *Clap your tiny...*

"Mummy, you awake now?" Bella asked, stopping mid-chorus when she saw her mother's eyes open. "Good," she said brightly and kissed Saffron's cheek. "Bella want juice." She slid off the bed and headed out the room.

Saffron stared ahead of her. The room was too bright; it hurt her eyes but she was afraid to blink. What if she couldn't open them again? She kept them open until they watered, quickly blinked and opened them wide again.

Oh, please somebody come in.

❧❦❧❦

"Daddy," Bella said groggily, sitting snuggled in her frothy pink princess bed as Lucas read her a story. Nico was already asleep in his bed shaped like a racing car across the room.

"Yes, babe?"

"Mummy has pretty eyes?"

"Mummy had the most beautiful eyes sweetheart," he answered softly, realizing his use of the past tense.

"Bella eyes yellow, Nico eyes yellow, Daddy eyes yellow, Mummy eyes brown!" said Bella.

Lucas stilled. The twins were just learning colours and described everything, but when had Bella seen her mother's eyes?

"You remember Mummy's eyes, Bella?"

"No, I sing to Mummy and she open eyes, then I got juice from Nana," she explained.

Lucas's heart thumped loudly in his chest as he tried to understand what his daughter was saying.

"You saw Mummy's eyes? Today?"

Bella nodded and stuck three fingers in her mouth sleepily.

"Today, Bella?" Lucas asked urgently.

Again Bella nodded drowsily, her eyelashes fluttering shut only to fly wide open when her father scooped her out of bed and strode with her down to her mother's bedroom.

"Tell her to open her eyes again, Bella?" Lucas ordered.

"No, Mummy sleeping."

"Please," he coaxed gently with a smile. He could always guarantee his daughter would show her stubborn side at the most inopportune moments.

"No, tomorrow we sing. G'night Daddy, night night Mummy." Bella closed her eyes and wrapped her chubby arms around Lucas's neck to settle her head in his shoulder.

Lucas sighed in frustration. Why did all the women in his life not do as they were told? he asked himself as he walked his head-strong daughter back to her bedroom, tucked her into bed and kissed her goodnight before going to sit with Saffron for the night.

⁂

"Bella saw Saffron's eyes open yesterday, Mama," Lucas said, trying to contain his excitement.

"What?"

"Bella said she saw Saffron's brown eyes yesterday,"

"When?"

"When indeed," Lucas drawled.

"She's always in and out of that room, Lucas. Let's just watch and see. If we make a production out of it Bella will refuse."

So they did nothing and one day slipped into the next.

Lucas was reading a book to Saffron one afternoon when Bella and Nico came in. He pretended to read and watched as the kids climbed onto the bed and talked to their mother.

Saffron didn't move and gave no indication of hearing them either.

"Daddy?" Bella said eventually.

"Yes, baby?"

"You come and sit here." Bella patted the bottom of the bed.

"Nico, you hold Mummy's hand and Mummy, you sing with me."

Clap your tiny hands
Clap your tiny hands...

Lucas didn't know the song but watched closely as his children interacted with their mother. His heart swelled with pride.

Jesus loves to hear...

Bella sang on, and then, like a regular occurrence, Saffron opened her eyes. Lucas sat frozen. He had waited for this moment for months, and he didn't know whether to laugh or cry. The moment seemed surreal. Not wanting to break the connection Saffron was having with the children, he slowly got up and turned down the louvred windows sending the room into shadow. The deep creases that had formed on Saffron's forehead immediately smoothed out.

"Keep singing for your mummy, Bella," Lucas said as he went to the doorway and called for Nurse Green and his mother.

They came and all surrounded the bed as Bella sang on and Nico clapped his hands. Saffron blinked once, twice, and then closed her eyes.

"Okay, Nana. Bella and Nico want juice pwease," Bella said.

With tears in her eyes, Nurse Green walked the children out of the room.

"Did you see, Mother?" Lucas asked, his voice husky with emotion. "She opened her eyes."

"I saw, my son," Doratea smiled, hugging him close. "Now talk to her while I ring the doctor." She closed the door as she left.

"Saff?" Lucas said nervously, "if you can hear me, blink once?"

He watched, but nothing happened and then felt a thousand joys as she opened her eyes and looked directly at him.

"Are you seeing me?" he asked. "Blink if you are?"

She blinked and he laughed and cried and gathered her up in his arms.

"Do you know who I am?"

Yes, you're Lucas, Saffron said to herself.

He watched her, but she said nothing.

Saffron closed her eyes and opened them again.

"You know me?"

She blinked and watched as his face lit up.

"You're coming back to us, Saff." Lucas gently kissed each of her eyelids, "You're coming back."

&ംഏ'ഴ-ൿ

Saffron was able to communicate through a series of blinks and eye movements and was beginning to remember more and more with each passing day.

Movement began with her toes and then in other places. Nurse Green worked her hard, but Lucas worked her harder. She would finish her recovery sessions with him bathed in sweat, exhausted and her muscles trembling. But Saffron didn't complain.

Her voice eventually came back and all that was keeping her from a full recovery was her ability to walk again.

&ംഏ'ഴ-ൿ

"What's this?" Saffron asked. The ring had been on her engagement finger when she woke from the coma nine weeks ago.

Lucas hovered near the doorway and Saffron watched fascinated as a tide of red crept up his neck and stained his cheeks.

"You probably don't remember me tell—ask—yeah ask you," Lucas stuttered, "but you agreed to marry me, just before Hurricane Maddox."

Saffron thought back, her brow furrowing as she tried to remember.

"It's probably in one of those gaps you can't remember," Lucas suggested. "I can hear Nico," he said suddenly backing into the hallway. "I'd better go." He rushed off.

Saffron watched him go and smiled looking down at the cluster of yellow and brown diamonds on her finger. The ring looked like it had been dipped in brown sugar. She loved it.

&~&~&

Saffron waved at Muzio, Doratea and the children as they set off down to the beach. Lucas had gone to Port Antonio on business and Nurse Green was off duty for an hour.

Saffron was sitting on a lounger, trailing her fingers in the pool. She'd just had her leg muscles massaged by a professional masseuse, and to keep her sore muscles from cramping, Nurse Green had dressed her in a soft flannel tracksuit. She was roasting in the late afternoon sun and couldn't wait to go inside, but she didn't have the energy to get herself there just yet.

Lucas and Saffron were due to be married in four days. A simple garden ceremony at the house with family and close friends. Saffron had hoped to walk down the aisle unaided, she didn't want to use a walking stick, although Doratea had decorated it in satin ribbon to match the wedding dress.

She was getting married! They were going to be a family. Saffron smiled as wide as a river and stretched her aching arms over her head, looking at the huge green hills to her right. Her smile faded and she lowered her arms as she watched a single grey cloud obscure the hill top. Saffron was suddenly reminded of the one thing she needed to do to make everything perfect.

&~&~&

Saffron was quietly catching some z's when a shadow blocked the sun in front of her, and a cold rough hand covered her mouth and nose, stifling her panicked scream.

"Scream and I will kill you now," said a voice she didn't recognise in a low menacing tone. She couldn't see the man's face.

"I see you managed to infiltrate my family and taint it with your nasty dark blood," the man said.

Saffron gasped as she finally recognised him. It was Lucas's father. He laughed bitterly, looming even closer. His silver hair was greasy, long and unkempt. His breath smelt of alcohol and his eyes were dark, flat and cold. Saffron knew she was looking at pure evil.

Try to remain calm, she told herself. The twins, Doratea and Muzio were safe if they stayed at the beach and Nurse Green was inside. It was her the old man wanted.

"Yes, you bitch, it's me," he sneered. "Get up. We're going for a little drive."

He moved his hand from her mouth slowly but pressed a long finger against her trembling lips, warning her to be quiet.

Grasping her arms, he tried to yank her up but Saffron's leg muscles were still recovering from all the exercise and wouldn't support her.

"I said get up!" he barked wildly, his soulless eyes darting about frantically. "I know what happened to you, and I wished you were dead. But yet again, I have to be the one to do it. It always comes down to me! Getting good help is so hard to find, and that son of mine is like his mother. Weak and pathetic! But my grandson," he said as his eyes narrowed and he licked his thin lips, "I will make him into a true Conti-Bridgewater and get rid of all that darkness in his blood!"

He was crazy, Saffron thought, trying hard not to react to his erratic words. He let her go suddenly and she fell heavily against the back support of the lounger. He was looking around madly and actually took two steps away from her. Saffron knew he was looking for Nico. But she decided she'd kill the old bastard first before he ever got near her son.

"Wait, I'll come!" she shouted. "I'll come but I need help." She lifted her hand and watched as his mouth twisted in distaste.

He straightened his wiry frame and walked over to her, watching her closely as he bent and placed his hands beneath her arms. She wrapped her arms around his neck and shifted to the end of the lounger. He pulled her hard and then tried to drag her off the seat, but he was weak and frail. He moved around to her other side to try again.

This time, he grabbed her upper arms and his bony fingers bit into her skin, almost cutting off her circulation. But Saffron ignored the pain and placed her palms on his flat chest. He was caught off guard. He wasn't prepared and stepped back, losing his balance.

He let her go as he tried to regain his balance. His thin arms waved frantically, windmill style, as his smooth shoes slipped on the edge of the pool. Suddenly, he flung himself forward and grabbed Saffron's hair before falling backwards into the water.

He didn't let go. Saffron fell to the floor and was dragged to the edge of the pool, her skin scraping painfully as she frantically tried to pry his bony fingers from her hair. But with a vicious yank, he dragged her into the water.

They both went under, creating a scene of tangled limbs, warm water and bubbles.

The old man was clawing at her wildly, trying to use her to lever himself out of the water. Saffron was rapidly sinking, the weight of the tracksuit quickly pulling her down. She touched the bottom and looked up, hearing the muffled sound of the old man's cries for help. Her legs were tired and useless, but she wanted to swim back up to help him, but she couldn't move.

Her lungs were bursting, her arms feeling heavy as she looked up and saw his face twisted in frozen panic, his mouth open as he stared at her blankly. Saffron closed her eyes and waited.

Lucas dropped his car keys on the table and casually walked with a spring in his step out to the pool, where everyone usually congregated at this hour of the day. He found it odd that he didn't hear any chatter or reggae music playing.

Suddenly, he saw a body floating in the water. With his heart beating madly, he ran to the pool, pulling off his shoes along the way, and dove straight in. He grabbed the body and turned it over, horrified to see his father's lifeless face, and for a split second he froze.

Then wiping the water out of his eyes, Lucas looked around, noticing movement and colour at the bottom of the pool. Taking a deep breath he dove under. He grabbed Saffron and hauled her out of the water. She wasn't breathing. He shouted for help as he loosened her clothing, covered her mouth with his and tried to revive her.

Saffron began coughing up water just as Nurse Green came out of the house, blood trickling from her temple.

"Are you all right?" Lucas asked the nurse.

She nodded, touching the small bump. "Someone hit me over the head." Lucas lifted Saffron and carried her to the house.

"Nurse Green, can you ring Muzio and tell him to come to the house, but leave the children with my mother please."

The nurse nodded, fishing into her pocket for her mobile phone and looking at the black suited body of a man floating in the pool.

Saffron followed her stare then buried her head in Lucas's shoulder.

"I'm sorry," she whispered as he placed her gently on the bed.

"I don't ever want to hear you say those words again." Lucas said, as tears began raining down his face.

Saffron put her arms around his broad shoulders and hugged him close as he cried. "It's all right. We're all safe now, Lucas." She squeezed him hard. "We're all safe now."

Much later, after the police had come and gone, and the old man's body taken away, Lucas walked into Saffron's bedroom wearing a plain white t-shirt and the old grey sweats she remembered from Nottingham.

His dark hair, damp from the shower he'd just taken, was flopping into his handsome face, and apart from the lines of strain around his eyes he looked at least ten years younger.

She smiled and took his hand. "Are you ok?"

Lucas thought for a moment, looking into her huge brown eyes. "I'm fine; it's you I'm worried about." He raked a hand through his hair. "You almost drowned! Should I get the doctor back?"

"Don't be silly. I'm fine. Just a little tired. That's all." She patted the space beside her on the bed. "Come and sit."

Knowing Lucas as well as she did, she knew he was probably beating himself up, thinking he should have prevented what had taken place today from happening.

"I didn't know he couldn't swim," Saffron said as he lay beside her, referring to his father. "He hated any form of weakness and obviously kept it to himself. He put a pool in every house he owned. But let's not talk about him. Are—" Saffron spoke before he could finish.

"If you are about to ask me how I'm feeling I think I will clobber you one." She sighed and stared at Lucas for a moment, wishing she could turn back time and love him again from the very beginning.

"Force of habit, I guess," Lucas said.

"There is one thing I would like you to do though."

"What's that?" Lucas asked

She reached up, put her fingers into his soft silky hair at his nape and pulled him down to her. It was their first proper kiss in almost eight months, and she put everything she was feeling for him into it.

Her lips played over his firm mouth and she flicked her tongue along the rim, dipping into his slight bow on the top then moving to nip at the corner of his mouth.

He groaned when she stabbed her smooth tongue into his mouth and she felt him smile as he finally opened up, letting her sweetly persuasive tongue in. She swept inside, deepening the kiss until her breasts felt heavy and her nipples peaked. The tension was building so fast and so intense that she let out a moan, pulling him down even further until their bodies touched from chest to toe. She sighed, feeling his stiff erection pressing against her thigh.

"We need to stop," Lucas said breathlessly, forcing himself away from her tantalizing mouth.

"Why?" Saffron asked gently as she sucked her finger and then swirled it around his ear.

"Because if we don't stop, I'll want to kiss you again and it won't stop there." He closed his eyes as she shifted her upper body closer to him, pressing her breasts into his chest so he could feel her nipples jutting out like hard pebbles against his warm skin.

"I don't want it to stop there," Saffron whispered seductively as she reached up and replaced her finger with her tongue, blowing softly into his ear.

"Are you sure?" Lucas asked, his eyes already full with desire. Saffron felt like the only woman on earth when he looked at her like that and her heart skipped a beat. She smiled, and threading her fingers in his long hair, urged him closer still.

"Your legs—"

"Are fine. Now come here," she ordered impatiently. The throbbing at her pelvis was intensifying, and she wanted and needed him to ease the pressure.

Lucas shifted and settled over her, careful not to put too much weight on her legs. The thin sheet was no barrier from the intense heat of their bodies, but he pushed it away anyway as he took over and kissed her deeply.

His hands travelled along her body, feeling the dips and curves as he moulded one soft breast with one hand while keeping his weight from her with the other.

Saffron moaned loudly, knowing he was holding back. She tried to take off her nightie, and before he realised what she was doing, she'd whipped it over her head, throwing it on the floor.

Her body had changed yet again, he noticed, thinner in some places, but her breasts were still bountiful and inviting. He dipped his head to suckle at her large ripe nubs, one and then the other, lapping at her peaks until they were stiff and pointy. He pushed her breasts together and nipped his teeth over them playfully until she moaned deep in her throat and moved sensually against him.

Saffron held onto his hair; she wanted him naked and made frustrated noises when she tried to lift his t-shirt so that she could touch his warm skin, but it was caught between their bodies and wouldn't shift.

With a huge grin, Lucas hauled off his shirt and settled between Saffron's legs, looking into her dark sensual eyes. He kissed her tenderly through the lace of her panties.

She bucked against his mouth, her hips lifting off the bed. He captured her bottom to hold her still as he nipped his teeth along her inner thighs, feeling her legs tremble as she tried to urge him on.

Lucas would not be rushed. With a slowness that made her scream he hooked his fingers into the sides of her panties and pulled them down her wonderfully long and smooth legs.

At the bottom of the bed, he took one of her tender feet in his palm and bestowed a tender kiss on each of her toes before smoothing his fingers along her delicate ankles and kissing the backs of each foot.

Saffron reached down and grabbed his hair trying to pull him up, but he held her wrists and kept them down on each side of her legs.

He moved up a little more, running his tongue along her shins to her knees until again he reached the only place she wanted him to be.

Saffron felt rigid as she waited. Her body was as taut as a bow string and became even tighter when he kissed her on the very spot she wanted him to.

She whimpered as he licked her, feeling the area between her legs swell against his tongue.

"Please," Saffron whispered, desperate to have him inside her.

Lucas looked up, his eyes as dark as hers. He held her gaze and watched her gasp as he placed one and then two fingers deep inside her.

Saffron closed her eyes, feeling the pressure mount as he thrust his fingers relentlessly. She clenched her inner muscles around them to intensify the feeling as she climbed to ecstasy.

In tune with every tremor, every breath and every gasp of her body, Lucas pumped his fingers faster until her body stiffened, but before she fell, he quickly shifted and replaced his fingers with his tongue, drinking her cream as she came and came.

Chapter Eleven

$\mathcal{I}$t was only right to cancel the wedding. Lucas didn't want to, but Saffron couldn't get married, knowing they hadn't buried Lucas's father yet. So they postponed the ceremony, and Lucas reluctantly flew to England to see to the burial.

The media had a field day. Things got ugly, but Lucas weathered it all with a ruthlessness that would have actually made his father proud. He signed the ugly London mansion over to a children's charity.

He never wanted to set foot into the damn place again. He sold his shares to the bank and the hotels, and what couldn't be sold he gave away. He was now a free man. He was going to Jamaica to do what he wanted, and nothing was ever going to separate him from his family again.

It took another two months before he was able to fly back down to the island, only a day before the wedding.

Lucas arrived at the house late, and went straight to the twins' room to stare at them, savouring all of their changes.

Bella was sprawled out on the bed with the sheets tangled around her chubby legs that looked longer. She'd grown. She still had her fingers in her mouth, he noticed affectionately. He kissed his daughter gently and covered her with another blanket.

Then Lucas slowly pulled the covers off the small mound in the centre of the other bed. Nico was a burrower. His son opened his sleepy eyes and looked at him.

"Hi, Daddy," he said sleepily, clutching his treasured elephant to his chest.

Lucas touched Nico's curly hair and smiled tenderly.

"Hi, son."

"We get married tomorrow?" Nico asked groggily.

Lucas grinned and kissed Nico's smooth cheek. "Yes, son, tomorrow we get married. Go back to sleep. See you in the morning."

"Night, night, Daddy."

"Good night, Nico."

"Love you, Daddy."

Lucas paused at the door and looked at his son closing his eyes and pulling the blankets over his head.

"I love you too, son." Lucas felt an overwhelming affection as he looked at his children before closing the door.

He walked down the narrow corridor, about to remove his tie that was no longer there. Lucas grinned at his foolishness. He had given away most of his ties, suits and silk shirts to charity.

He walked past Saffron's bedroom door, then stopped. His mother would flay him if she knew he tried to see his bride the night before the wedding. But what the heck, he thought, he hadn't seen his future wife in weeks. All he wanted was one quick peek.

He knew Saffron was still doing physio, and she'd been very cagey on the phone when they talked about her legs. He didn't care if she was in a wheelchair. He loved her and was a little disappointed that she could think that the state of her legs would matter to him. Or maybe she didn't love him. Lucas felt a sharp dart pierce his heart at the thought, knowing that he had bullied her into marrying him. She'd never actually told him that she loved him.

Stealthily he looked up and down the dimly lit corridor and pushed open the door.

Saffron lay asleep on her side. He watched her lovingly before kissing her softly on the forehead and removing his soft loafers, which dropped silently on the marble floor.

"Where do you think you're going, Gianluca?" Saffron asked sleepily.

He turned around and tiptoed over to her, noticing that for the first time she had used his real name. He hadn't realised how much it meant to him until she'd said it. It was as though he could be himself now and not hide ever again. He loved it. He wanted her to say it again and again.

"Hi." He knew he was grinning like an idiot, but Lucas couldn't help himself. "I didn't mean to wake you."

"Yes, you did," Saffron teased, pulling herself up to lean against the wooden headboard. "Aren't you going to kiss me properly?"

"No."

"No?"

"I've been in the same clothes for a day. I need to shower," Lucas said.

"Don't be silly."

"But I just might allow myself to be taken advantage of the night before I get married though. I'm sure my future wife wouldn't mind."

"Well, I'm sure your future bride won't mind me sampling her groom for her." Saffron said. "One kiss, then I'll let you go."

Lucas pretended to think about it by tapping one long lean finger against his chin, while his golden eyes danced with mischief. He then walked over and leaned down to kiss her gently.

It was more a brushing of lips, and Saffron was quick to wrap her arms around his neck and pull him down to her.

"When did you become so assertive," he mumbled against her mouth as he settled beside her.

"Since I've been starving for you all these weeks. Now shut up and kiss me properly."

Lucas laughed quietly and obeyed. His kiss sent sweet sensations throughout her body, making her nipples peak. She curved her body sensually into his.

He moaned and tried to pull away, but she wasn't having it.

Saffron pulled and he fell with suspicious ease on top of her, and then it was her turn to gasp as his warm tongue trailed down her long neck and his hands moved over her body.

"We shouldn't," Lucas murmured as he pushed her simple top aside and captured a nipple in his warm mouth. She tasted so good, he thought to himself, as he hungrily lapped at her breast.

Saffron held his head, caressing the soft length of his hair as she tugged slightly and offered him her other breast.

"We really shouldn't do this," he mumbled again, moving down her body to tickle her belly button with his tongue.

"Oh yes, we should." Saffron gasped when his fingers reached under her soft jersey shorts and touched her secret place.

Shifting slightly, she turned and undid the buttons on his brightly coloured shirt, sliding a knowing hand through his wiry chest hair.

Her mouth was level with his left nipple and she nibbled at it, delighting when he groaned. She nibbled it again and again until it became pebble hard.

Moving her hand lower, Saffron cupped him through his jeans, loving the feel of his huge penis pushing urgently against her hand, and with a knowing smile and another tug on his nipple, she cupped his scrotum before gripping the hot pulsating length of his manhood, moving her hand up and down.

She pushed him onto his back, giving herself easier access. Their forearms crossed between their bodies as they touched each other intimately.

Lucas's fingers moved deep within her, his thumb rubbing against her clitoris with each thrust of his hand.

Saffron's hand gripped his throbbing member even tighter and moved even faster, thrilled by her power to give him pleasure while his hips moved in jerking movements.

Their bodies grew tense at the same time. Saffron moved faster and sucked his nipple hard as his warm seed spilled into her waiting hand.

His body jerked twice, but he didn't stop moving his fingers within her until, burying her cries in his sweaty neck, she reached her climax.

"Gianluca!" she sobbed as she fell helpless in his arms.

It took a while for the two of them to recover. Lucas was first and reached over to the bedside table, turned on the lamp and grabbed a couple of tissues to clean them both up. Once finished, he lay down and gazed into her eyes, smiling.

"You are amazing," Saffron whispered, turning to face him.

"And you are insatiable. What's in your hand?" he asked, noticing her clenched fist before they had started making love.

"You'll laugh," she mumbled and tried to move away.

"I won't," he promised, leaning down to kiss her nose. "Please?"

Slowly, Saffron opened her hand, and there sitting in the centre of her palm was the tiny fairy holding up a flower that Lucas had given her years ago.

He looked down at it, and then looked up at Saffron, his eyes smouldering with love. He kissed her gently.

"I love you too," he whispered.

⊱•✿•⊰

"Saffron, you have a visitor," Doratea said, walking into the room. "Oh my! You look so beautiful." Doratea wiped a tear from her eye as she looked at Saffron wearing a long, strapless satin dress the exact shade as chilled champagne.

"Doratea, if you cry then I will cry and we'll have to do my make-up again," Saffron sniffed, smiling. "But thank you. I hope Gianluca will like it."

"Gianluca won't be able to keep his hands off you if last night was something to go by," Doratea said and raised a knowing grey eyebrow sternly, but then began laughing.

Saffron flushed with embarrassment. "Who's the visitor?" she asked. She'd had breakfast with her mother and Mas Arthur in the morning, and Roderick and his friend Jefferson had arrived over an hour ago. She frowned trying to figure out who the person could be.

"I'll go and fetch."

"Okay."

Saffron was putting her earrings on when the door swung open again. She looked at the visitor through the mirrored reflection on the dresser. She spun around and froze.

"Cass?" she asked in disbelief with a flurry of movement, they were crying and hugging, laughing and crying some more.

"How did...where did you come from?" Saffron asked through her tears.

"I flew in with Gianluca yesterday, but stayed with Miss Hyacinth last night," Cassidy explained, wiping the tears from her huge blue-grey eyes.

Saffron held Cassidy's hands and looked at her.

Cassidy's blonde hair was loose and trailing over one shoulder. She was wearing soft pink lip gloss and mascara and a light blue silk dress that stopped just above her knees. She had on strappy heels.

"You look amazing."

"Thanks," Cassidy said and glanced down at herself and shrugged in a way that was achingly familiar to Saffron. The friends hugged again.

"I'm really sorry, Cass. I was such a bitch, and I know that I–"

Cassidy stopped her before she could finish.

"No. I was too dependent on you, Saffron. I needed to spread my wings and be by myself for a while."

"Did you–" Saffron was afraid to ask, but Cassidy knew what she was trying to say.

"He's here." Cassidy beamed.

"Here?"

"He's taller than me, speaks better English than me and dying to meet you."

"Billal? You found him? Where was he all this time? What happened?"

Cassidy glanced down at her simple silver watch then at the closed bedroom door. "Gianluca said I only had five minutes," Cassidy replied anxiously.

"A few more minutes won't hurt him." Saffron sat on the edge of the bed and folded her arms in a pose that said she was not going to move until she was good and ready.

"Okay," Cassidy breathed in deeply. "But this is the edited version. I went to India, didn't find him. Went back to Nottingham, got the compensation cheque and did a business course. Gianluca gave me a job. Then I went back to India to one of his hotels and interviewed a boy for a shoe polishing job. It was like looking into the male version of me. It was easy to piece together after that.

"Just like that? He came to you?"

Cassidy nodded. "Tarif had taken him to India and was killed in a car accident the next day. Before he died he'd told the British Embassy what he'd done, gave them my name, but somehow it went wrong from there. They couldn't trace me, and Billal was sent to an orphanage run by British nuns in Mumbai."

"Oh, Cass, I'm so glad you didn't listen to me and didn't give up. Being a mother, I now understand. I'd search the world for my babies forever if I had too." Saffron took her friend's hand and squeezed. They didn't need anymore words to explain what they were both feeling.

"Ok, enough about me." Cassidy stood and hugged her friend. "Gianluca will be banging on the door any minute now if I don't get out of here!" Cassidy smiled brightly. Saffron had never seen her friend look so radiant. "It's taken you and Gianluca way too long to get to this place. But I'm so glad."

Doratea and Bella knocked on the door a few minutes later after Cassidy left.

"It's time, Saffron."

Taking Bella's hand,w they walked out into the evening sunshine.

177

Gianluca turned as the steel drummer began to play the wedding march. Bella, wearing a long gold and cream dress that looked as though it had come straight out of one of her storybooks, walked towards him with her adorable face scrunched up in concentration as she counted her steps and threw petals onto the white aisle.

The sun caught the sparkling gold crown balancing precariously on her dark curls, and Gianluca felt his heart leap as he watched his baby girl.

Then Saffron came out and his heart stopped completly. He watched her walk towards him with the aid of a cane outrageously decorated in ribbon. She was smiling brightly, her eyes so clear and sparkling that she took his breath away. She was the most beautiful woman he had ever seen.

Then, as the music stopped, she looked around and then gave him a look he couldn't interpret. Their wedding guests all turned to see what was going on and watched with bated breath.

The collar of his shirt felt suddenly tight. She had changed her mind, Lucas thought in panic. He was about to drag her up to the altar when Bella blocked his path and clung to his legs.

"Wait, Daddy," she whispered and reached around him to give her basket to her Nana. "Hit it!" she shouted to the drummer and then ran to the altar to stand beside her brother, who was the best man.

Lucas watched in shock as Saffron sent him a saucy wink, threw down the cane and danced up the aisle to Will Smith's "Getting jiggy with it", with her hips swaying and her arms drifting over her head as she danced towards him.

Lucas flung his head back and laughed before moving out to meet Saffron half-way, lifting her up and kissing her long and hard as the guests clapped and cheered.